I0553078

Softening Lyric

Copyright

Disclaimer

The books in this series are based completely on dreams that I've had or that one of the other people in my relationship has had. They all have a little bit of real life thrown in so that you, the reader, can get to know us a little bit better.

These books can and should be read as standalone books. There isn't an order to them. All of the characters in the books are the same, as they are all based on characters from real life.

As you read these books, please keep in mind that other than the characters and the city they are based in, these books are not connected to other books in the series. They aren't a continuation of other books. They are all novellas based on dreams that revolve around the same characters.

As you keep that in mind, please enjoy reading this book. I do hope you will also read the others in this series and love them as much as I loved writing them!

Opening Quote

I am not ashamed anymore, I want something so impure. You better impress now, watching my dress now fall to the floor. Crawling underneath my skin, sweet talk with a hint of sin. Begging you to take me. Devil underneath your grin, sweet thing. But she play to win. Heaven gonna hate me.

Not Afraid Anymore by Halsey

Chapter One

☆ Lyric ☆

(Two Years Ago)

I climb into the passenger side of our squad car and let out a long, heavy sigh as I close my eyes. I rub my temples a moment before pulling my shoulder length auburn hair up into a messy bun. Tears sting my eyes, but I refuse to show them. I won't. I really can't. Not in my profession.

Being a constable for the Hertfordshire Constabulary is something I've wanted to do ever since I was a young child. I've never wanted to be anything else. Being accepted to work for the Constabulary is one of my greatest accomplishments. I worked hard to get where I am. There aren't many female constables. It's always been a man's job. I wasn't going to let that stop me.

I've always been one to crash through the glass ceiling. I've never let anything hold me back. It's not in my nature. My nana always told me that if I put my mind to it, I could be Queen of England. Heritage and bloodlines be damned. She said the entire commonwealth would fall at my feet. The Royal Military would be at my side.

It was one of the only things that got me through some incredibly tough times in my life. My nana had always been my biggest fan. Her words got me through all of the bullying in school. Her hugs got me through the hurtful words my brother threw at me. The jabs my mother uttered under her breath when she didn't think I'd hear. It was my nana's belief in me that I could do anything, be anything, that got me here.

Losing her was devastating. Crushing. Like the very air I breathe was sucked from my lungs. I no longer had her as a barrier between the ugliness that is the rest of my family. I no longer had my shield. I was exposed. And it was hard for a little while. But her voice always came back to me. It's like she's the little angel in my ear that tells me to get back up. Keep going. Follow my dreams.

"Ready to get out of here?" The deep male voice next to me pulls me out of my reverie. I look over slowly at him and give him a weak smile. My trainer, Tyler Jackson, is really a rather amazing man. He's kind of become like a father to me. He's about twenty years older than my twenty-seven years. I started my law enforcement career late.

After I lost my nana, I spent a lot of time trying to keep my life from derailing. I had to learn how to deflect all of the negativity thrown at me from those supposed to love me. When I finally picked myself up and dusted myself off, I decided hiding away and not living my life is not at all who I am. I refused to let my nana down.

"Yeah. Yeah. I'm ready."

Tyler nods and starts driving, glancing at me ever so often as we patrol. He's not used to me being so quiet. "You plan on telling me what's going on? I can't help but notice how quiet you've been the last few days."

I glance at him. For a man nearly fifty, Tyler Jackson is rather attractive. His hair hasn't begun to gray yet. It's still a lighter brown. He's clean-shaven. He's tall. Over six feet at least. His arms bulge as he steers.

I sigh. "It's... Hamilton."

"Prescott?" He looks at me with a raised and questioning eyebrow.

I stare straight ahead. "Yeah. He's... been bothering me. A lot."

"How do you mean?"

"He asked me out. I went out with him once, but... he was so boring. He droned on and on about himself and his family. How they own Prescott Winery. I don't even like wine. It's so... blech. Then he started

going on about how he's got a trust fund and what he's done with it. All of his trips. Like that would make him more attractive somehow. I couldn't get a word in edgewise. And if I'm being completely honest... he smelled like onion crackers and garlic. Ick." I dramatically shudder.

Tyler makes a face. "That's disgusting."

I scrunch my nose. "And body odor."

Tyler laughs. "You know we've actually written him up for that?"

My eyes widen. I snap my head to him. "Can you technically tell me that?"

He shrugs and winks. "So what's happened that has you so down? You really wishing that date would've worked out?"

"Oh fuck no. I mean, sure. It would've been nice to hit it off with someone, but... not him. No. The problem is that the date was near the beginning of training. And since then he's..." I shudder and shake my head. "He's becoming... I don't know... creepy?" I struggle to find the right word to describe it.

"Creepy? What is he doing to make him creepy?"

"Waiting by my locker after his shift is over for mine to start. He keeps bringing me flowers and leaving them for me. They end up wilted. I told him I hate flowers. He keeps relentlessly asking me out. I've told him no. The other day he demanded I go to the Fox Pub. I didn't. I went home. He got really mad at me. He was yelling and screaming at me in the locker room. And... I'm pretty sure he followed me home last night."

"What? Why am I just hearing about this?"

I shrug. "I really didn't think it was a big deal," I say quietly. "Until this morning. He was waiting for me by my locker. He said he was sick and tired of me playing this hard to get game with him. He said he knew I wanted him. That he's never not been able to get what he wants." I take a deep breath as I roll up my sleeve to my upper arm and unbutton the top two buttons of my uniform.

Tyler looks at my arm. "Holy shit. Did he touch you?"

I hesitate then move my collar down and tilt my neck to the side. "Yeah. I'd say he did."

Tyler pulls onto the side of the road and reaches over to pull my collar down slightly more to get a better view. "Fuck. You're filing a report. Now, Lyric."

7

I shake my head as I start buttoning up and arranging my uniform. "I can't do that."

He turns the squad around. "Then I'll do it on your behalf. I'm not letting that fucker get away with this."

One of the things I truly respect about Tyler is his overwhelming sense of justice and protection. He doesn't let anything get by him. And he's always been protective of me and other officers. It's who he is. Opening up to him has never been hard for me because he's so easy to talk to, and I know he'll listen.

But I've kept this quiet for so many reasons. I've always felt weak. Less than nothing. It's how I was treated by my brother. By his friends. By people I thought were my friends. By just about everyone. Becoming a police officer is my way of saying fuck all of that. I'm not weak. I can rise above all of that. I can take care of myself. And above everything, I can be that person who stands up for others. I can be their voice when they can't speak. Their legs when they can't stand. I can be for them what I didn't have for me.

"I don't want to cause any problems," I say softly as Tyler speeds back to our station.

"You aren't the one causing problems. He's causing problems." Tyler whips into the parking lot and gets out. He bends and looks in the car when I don't move. "You coming?"

"Fuck no. Are you crazy? That's his car right there. He's still here. I just started my shift, and he's already waiting for me."

"All the more reason for you to be with me. Move it."

I sigh, cursing him under my breath, but do what I'm told. I follow him into the station only to be greeted by a glare when Hamilton sees me. I stand tall, refusing to withdraw into myself. I won't let him have that power. I won't let anyone have that power. Never again. I'm not stupid enough to not admit to myself that standing behind Tyler gives me more strength then I'd have otherwise, though.

"My office, Prescott. Now." I watch with a small amount of satisfaction at the fear that passes over Hamilton's face as he follows Tyler to his office.

The seconds turn into minutes as I stand against a wall with my arms folded over my chest staring at the door to Tyler's office. Giving up on the idea of standing any longer, I sit in an office chair and twirl in a circle as I keep glancing at the door, willing the entire ordeal to be over with so he'll hopefully stop bothering me. I doubt I'll be that lucky, but a girl can dream, can't she?

After what seems to me like hours upon hours, Tyler's door opens. Hamilton shoots me a furious death ray through his eyes as he storms out of the station. I hold back the flinch and lower my eyes as Tyler follows, making sure he leaves.

Tyler turns towards me and gestures for me to follow him to his office. After filling out mounds of paperwork regarding Hamilton and all of his harassment at work and not, Tyler releases me from duty for the rest of the day.

I decide to take advantage of the nice day and go for a drive. Sometimes solitude is the best way to get my mind back in the right frame. And then a nice bath with a good book. Perfect way to end any day.

My plans are ruined with epic proportions, though, when I pull onto my street. There's a flurry of activity. Fire trucks everywhere. Of course, I can't tell exactly where they are, but I don't need to. I know instinctively as soon as I see Hamilton Prescott's car that it's mine.

"Oh my God..." I'm sick to my stomach. I'm dizzy. The world tilts on its axis. I feel like I'm standing on my head watching all of the events unfold as I come to a stop in front of my house. My... house.... My nana's house. I inherited it. It was... one of the last few things I had left of her.

One of... I can't breathe. I don't recall getting out of my car. I don't recall walking towards the house. Or getting around anyone who was there. I don't remember anything but the flames suddenly surrounding me. I don't even register when Tyler's arms wrap around me from behind. He lifts me as he pulls us both away from the flames. I don't know how much I fight to get free. To get into the house. To save the very few things I cherish. Nor do I register what I say to him. Scream to him. I can't hear his voice at first. The way he is speaking softly. Clearly. It's not until he turns my face to look at him, focus on him, that I even realize he's there.

"Lyric." His hands are on each side of my face. I blink a few times. "Lyric. Come on. Focus."

I shake my head like I'm coming out of a smoky haze. My trembling hands are gripping his wrists. My nails are digging into his skin, but I can't force myself to let go. "Why... would... he... do... this?"

9

He slowly shakes his head as he keeps his green eyes on me. "I don't know. I don't know, Lyric. I got here as quick as I could. I was on my way home. You know I don't live far away. I saw the flames. I came up here to check on you. I saw Hamilton. He was just about to get in his car. I jumped out and chased him but lost him."

I shatter. I fall to the ground and curl into a tight ball crying. I feel Tyler wrap his strong arms around me and rock me back and forth on the cold cement ground. I scream as my house, the only home I've ever known, explodes behind me. Ashes and flaming embers rain down around us.

Gone.

Everything.

My whole life.

He took my whole life.

I have nothing now.

Nothing.

(Present Day)

I jerk awake, sitting up in the bed, drenched in sweat. My skin is dripping. My sheets are soaked. My covers are strewn haphazardly across the bed. I gasp for breath as I cry. My tears mix with the perspiration as I grip at my chest. I haven't made an attempt to open my eyes. I don't want to see where I am. I don't want to see the flames surrounding me. Licking at my skin. Waiting to consume me.

It takes a few minutes to realize that the sheets I'm gripping in my other hand aren't on fire. I slowly open my eyes, whimpering and trembling. The cool air conditioned air in my apartment hits my skin. I shiver. I slowly let go of the sheet and my chest and hug myself.

"Holy shit. Oh fuck." I come back to myself as I blink myself awake. I look at my clock. "Five." Time for work. I shakily get out of my bed and trip, falling hard to the ground. "Fuck you, stupid ground." I push myself up and limp to the bathroom, rubbing my wrist. I turn the shower on and let the water run.

10

After I'm done with my shower and dressed, I grab my equipment and head to my car. I slowly climb in and turn my air conditioner on as I drive to Gainesville Police Department's Headquarters.

The drive into work is peaceful. Quiet. The sun rising over Gainesville, Florida, paints the sky brilliant pinks and, my favorite, purples. Despite the early morning hour, the heat of the day is already setting in. The July sun is hot. Even with the air conditioner on, I can feel the sun permeating into my skin, warming my insides. I can't decide if that's a good thing or a bad thing. After that dream… I shake my head and shiver, even though I feel warm. I've been having those dreams more and more lately.

When I first moved here, a little over a year ago, I fell in love with the beauty of this city. The warmth and kindness of its people. It's different than anywhere in Harpenden, the city I lived in while in the United Kingdom. People are cold. Aloof. Better than everyone else.

I pull into the police parking garage and park my car, taking a few deep breaths to steady myself as I get out. I grab my gear and head for the locker room to finish dressing for my shift. I beeline to my locker, keeping my head down and hoping no one notices the bags under my eyes. Especially…

"Hey, Lyric!" a far too perky as shit for this time of the morning voice says behind me.

I close my eyes and sigh quietly. Especially her. I plaster on my best fake smile as I turn to her. "Hey, Mariah!" I say as cheerfully as I can.

She furrows her eyebrows and pulls me on the bench next to her. "What's wrong? Another dream?"

I hate that she can always see right through me. I've never been able to keep anything from her. She's like a human lie detector. And she can sense when anything is wrong. I should've known better.

I let out a breath. "Yeah. It was about being in Harpenden. The night he burned my house down."

"Oh, Lyric…" She immediately hugs me, and I feel instantaneously comforted. "I hate that you're still having these dreams. It's been nearly two years since it happened. Have you heard anything from him at all?"

I subtly bite my lip and close my eyes, burying my face in her shoulder and gripping the long dark, silky hair she hasn't put up for our

11

shift yet. "No." It's a lie. He's calling me. I think. I really don't know. Just... strange calls. Nothing to bring up. Not now. I can take care of it.

"What about Tyler? Has he heard anything about where Hamilton disappeared to?"

I shake my head. "He's a ghost. But he wouldn't know I'm here. And it's different now. This time I have more back-up. Even if he does find me." I give her a squeeze and shove all of my worries and fears back down deep inside where they belong.

Mariah pulls away and looks with concern at me. I can tell she knows I'm holding something back. She always knows. I focus on the silver speck in her deep blue eyes before looking away. If I don't, I'll tell her everything. I don't want her to be put in any danger if my suspicions are true.

"You'll always have backup," she says.

"Who needs backup?" a deep timber with a Southern twang asks from behind me. I'd jump, but I'd recognize the voice anywhere. I never thought I would ever say it, but thank God for DJ Rens. Thank God he showed up now to save me from the inquisition I instinctively know she's about to start.

I turn and give him a genuine smile. "Hey, DJ. How's your day?"

"Well, it was going great. Then I lost my partner. Figured she'd be back here with the second prettiest girl in the department." He smiles cockily as he winks at Mariah.

She blushes a deep red as she stands. "Let's just go, Rens. I don't want the entire department to know I'm another notch in your bedpost." He grabs her arm and leans down, looking around. He whispers something I can't hear in her ear and kisses her neck. She laughs and shoves him away.

The difference between the two of them is almost unbelievable, but they make it work. DJ is really tall. Something close to six feet three or over . He's built of solid steel. He has jade colored eyes and short dark-brown, spiked hair and light stubble on his face. He doesn't have curves. He has sharp ridges and lines. Women constantly fall at his feet.

It's fun to watch him ignore all of them, though, because he only has eyes for Mariah. She doesn't come near his height. She's barely five feet three. For every line and ridge of his body, for every muscle, she has soft curves. He could wrap himself around her and not a single hair on her head would be seen.

DJ looks over at me. "How's training? You're almost done, right?"

"Fuck. Finally. Feels like it's taking forever."

"It was like that for me, too," he says.

"Just be lucky you guys didn't have my trainer." Mariah pouts cutely. DJ and I both laugh.

"I've heard horror stories from other people, too," I laugh again.

"Oh, come on now. Matt isn't that bad. I trained him, and I'm awesome." DJ waves his hand arrogantly at himself giving us both teasing smiles.

Mariah looks up at him, mock surprised. "Are you saying Lieutenant Matt Chance is... actually not a bad guy?"

DJ laughs. "He's a fucking prick. But that's why I like him."

"Because you're a fucking prick?" I tease.

His eyes widen, and he attempts to give us an innocent look. "Me? I'm a fucking Saint." We all laugh as DJ looks at his watch. "Time to save Gainesville from speeding college kids and drunk old ladies."

I shake my head and look at him confused. "Don't you mean drunk college kids and speeding old ladies?"

Mariah shakes her head as DJ takes her hand and turns. "Nope. After the day we had yesterday, he definitely means speeding college kids and drunk old ladies."

DJ throws a wink at me as he leads Mariah out of the locker room. I smile as they both wave. I finish getting ready and hurry to follow them both to the turnout room. A huge smile spreads across my face. I'm eager to get this week over with. Soon I'll actually be on my own. That's further than I got in the United Kingdom, and I'll be damned if I let Hamilton Prescott ruin this for me.

Chapter Two

☆ Matt ☆

I let out a long breath as I start taking my gear off. I love my job. Being a cop is something I've wanted to do for a long time. Maybe not my whole life. I was a truly rebellious kid. I got in trouble. A lot. My parents discussed shipping me off to military school at one point. They probably would've kicked me out, though. I've never been that great with authority, and I didn't understand the idea behind military school. If I don't listen to my parents, why they hell would I listen to some asshole barking orders at me?

I put my duty belt in my bag and slip on jeans and a black t-shirt, putting my gun on my desk so I can slip my belt on. It's a good fucking thing I'm a Lieutenant with the Gainesville Police Department now. It means I don't have to go out on patrol unless I'm needed. And I better not be needed today.

I'm also a commander with our SWAT team. And last night we had one hell of a call. I was just getting ready for bed when it came in. A mental health crisis that patrol officers had been dealing with for several hours. It turned deadly. He got a hold of a gun and shot at someone in the house. We later found out it was his father.

After seven hours of SWAT being there, on top of the five that patrol had been there just talking to him and trying to get him to come down, we entered the house.

I put my gun in its holster and scrub my hands down my face. This is going to be a super long day. I can already feel it. At least I don't have to leave my office. It's the one thing that might get me through this fucking day.

I look up at the knock on my door. "Hey, Matt. Come to my office. We need to talk. Nice save today, by the way."

"Thanks, Brody," I grumble as I clip my badge to my belt. It was a good save, but it was only on my command. I was out in the fucking truck manning surveillance because my usual guy who would be doing that got sick and had to go home. And when I say sick… I really mean sick. Like not pretty kind of sick. Puking in the bush, making disgusting sounds from parts of his body that I didn't know could make sounds. I didn't send him home because I took pity. I sent him home because he almost made me puke watching him.

I sent my entrance team in right before the sun came up. It had been quiet for a while. He'd shot at us. He'd shot erratically at neighboring homes we'd evacuated. We entered after it had been quiet for over an hour. No response to any of our attempts at communicating. Nothing. We didn't know if he'd shot himself and needed help, if he was lying in wait for us to enter, or if he had fallen into a state of exhaustion and went to sleep.

In the end, he'd fallen asleep. Deeply. He woke up when he was being arrested and was so confused about what was happening to him that he put up no fight at all. Easiest takedown I think my team has ever had since I've been a commander. And the best news is that his father is going to live, though we weren't sure about that for most of the time we were there.

I rub the grit from my eyes and tap my cheeks a few times to wake myself up a little before I head to my Captain's office. I'll have to make a trip to the bathroom and splash cold water on my face.

The fucked up thing about being a SWAT commander and a Lieutenant is that if I have a SWAT call the night before, I'll still have to go to work and work my regular duties no matter how long the call takes. It's true for all my guys and girls. If they work a shift the next day, they need to show up for it. We simply don't have the staff to give them a day off and get it covered.

Something I've been fighting to change. We don't have enough officers for our call volume or our city's population. While the command staff agrees with me, our city management absolutely does not. Instead of getting us the budget we need to function properly, they'd rather make sure they have their houses in the Bahamas. Salary caps for us. Raises for them every damn year.

I knock on the doorframe of Brody's office door. He looks up at me from his desk and motions me in. I nearly collapse in a chair as I wait for him to finish whatever he's doing and tell me what the hell he wants. I have a plan for today. My plan is to go over reports from my SWAT call and spend the rest of the day doing whatever paperwork I need to do.

"Brent is out on injury. He broke his ankle in the gym after shift last night." Brody looks up at me.

I narrow my eyes. "So? What does that have to do with me?"

He points his pen at me. "It means you need to pick up where he left off with his trainee. Lyric Sharpe. All the other trainers have their own trainees or they have other assignments."

I shake my head and stand. "Fuck no. No. I'm fucking exhausted. You know how long I was out on that call. You want me to go out there and not only patrol, but also train someone? No fucking way."

"You don't have a choice, Chance. We have no one else. Sergeant Rens was out just as long as you, and he just went out on patrol."

"He doesn't have to train a new loudmouth, thinks-she-knows-everything-because-she-was-a UK-cop brat!" I stand and angrily pace back and forth across the office as Brody watches me.

"First. If you believe a word that just came out of your mouth, then you don't know a damn thing about her. Second. You're the best, Matt. I wouldn't ask you to step in otherwise."

I growl as I pace. His tone throws me, and it pisses me off more. It's almost like he knows something I don't. Like he knows something about Lyric that he's keeping from everyone else. Why that puts me on edge is something I'm not a hundred percent sure of, and I always trust my instincts.

It's really not that I have an issue training. I don't. I have an issue training her. She's loud. She disobeys. She thinks she knows all of our

16

policies and procedures because she was a cop who never got through her training in the United Kingdom. She moved here, probably because she thought it would be easier. She has another thing coming.

I finally stop pacing and turn to him. "Fine, Brody. But I'm not going easier on her just because she's a woman from another country. I'm not going to tolerate the shit that she's gotten away with up until now. I don't know if it's because Brent thinks she's hot or what the hell, but I won't tolerate blatant insubordination. She listens, or I'm done. I stop her training. She can get shipped back to the UK for all I care."

"I know you're crabby because you're tired, and you don't want to leave the office today, but don't go out there with that attitude, or you'll face me. I'm not in the mood for your shit today."

I glare at him, but shut my mouth. Brody is only about ten years older than my thirty-nine years, but he's a mentor. He's more than that. He's like a father figure. I know I can count on him for anything I need in my career or my personal life.

I take a deep breath. "Where is she?"

"In the turnout room waiting for you."

"Fuck, this isn't going to end well," I mutter to myself as I stride out of the office. I head for mine to grab my cuffs and memo pad with a pen. "Not going to end well at all." I walk with a damn near childish stomp to the turnout room before stopping myself from acting like an immature five-year-old. I close my eyes a second before stepping into the room.

Sitting in the middle of the room with her head down in her arms is a small woman with beautiful auburn hair that hits just past her shoulders. I would know her anywhere. I don't even need to see her face.

Part of the reason I don't want anything to do with being stuck in a car with her for ten hours of my day is because I'm already insanely attracted to her. I've done all I can to avoid her at all costs, and I've been doing a damn good job.

"Fuck," I whisper as I rub my temples. I steel myself with a low growl as I walk towards her. "Lyric." It's gruffer than I intended. I wince a little when she jumps and looks up at me. "Brent is out with an injury so you're stuck with me. Grab your gear. Let's move." I turn before she has a chance to stand and start walking to the garage.

"Asshole," she says under her breath, unaware that I can still hear her.

17

I let out another low growl. I hear the chair scrape across the floor and her grabbing her gear as she storms after me. I keep my stride long and quick, forcing her to damn near run to keep up. She's only around five feet four. She's a foot shorter than I am. With a sexy as hell perky little ass I can't stop thinking of spanking. And tits that her uniform shirt does nothing to hide. Fuck if I wouldn't give anything to bury my face in them.

I make my way to the garage, shooting a withering stare at anyone who dares look in my direction. I have to get this ridiculous fucking attraction under control. There's a reason I don't date. I not only have very picky tastes, but I have extremely particular bedroom likes. I pick my women up in a particular secret club and never see them again after I'm through with them.

She's a relationship type of person. One night would never be enough for her. And, unfortunately for me, I'd never be able to let her go after one night. Which pisses me off even more. I don't like the way I feel around her. She's a brat. Nowhere near submissive enough for me. I doubt she'd let me dominate her in any manner. Let alone the bedroom. I can't envision her backing down to anyone.

Which is one of the things I have to reluctantly admit makes her a hell of a cop. Fuck that she's not through with training yet. I've read her file. I've seen her in action, though she probably doesn't know that. She's the only one in her class who stood up to me in the tactics part of it. The only one who managed to listen to me enough to be able to take me down.

If I'm being honest, I admire the hell out of the girl. She's tenacious. Fierce. She's got a fire; a passion that I've only seen in a few other cops I've trained. Her skills really are unparalleled. Her only problem is that she doesn't think before she acts. She's reckless. It's something that she needs to fix before I'll even consider passing her.

I open the passenger side door to her assigned squad and glance back at her as she closes the trunk after putting her gear in it. She looks at me bewildered.

"What?"

"Brent... He drove. I... always rode shotgun."

I shake my head and turn, sliding in the passenger seat. "You're in your eleventh week of training. You should've been driving in your sixth." I close the door behind me. A few moments later, she quietly opens the door and starts to get in. "Stop."

She pauses and looks at me. "What?"

"You didn't do your vehicle safety check. Didn't check any fluids. Lights. Nothing."

"Brent always -"

"I don't care if Brent always did it. You're going to be in a squad by yourself very soon. Do your check. Do it right. Or we don't leave the garage, and I give you paperwork to do the rest of the day."

She shoots me a glare with a pout and sniffles as she slams the door. "Jerk."

I watch her intensely as she performs the check like I told her to, checking each thing off the list before putting the clipboard between the seats as she slides in. She doesn't say a word to me as she adjusts the mirrors. She glares at me as she puts her seat belt on and waits for me to do the same. I click it in and adjust it as she backs out.

She pulls out onto the street and begins her patrol. I turn the squad's laptop towards me. "You didn't check for any pending calls."

"I've done everything else wrong. Figured I'd add to the list."

I give her a grunt in response. Her British accent is driving me crazy. All I can think about is kissing her. "There's a disturbance on Village Drive. We'll take that first."

"Whatever." She heads towards the call.

"When we get there, it'll probably be done. You're going to end up dealing with angry people because we didn't show up as it was happening. It looks like it was probably a noise complaint and squads had more important calls. You'll need to calm -"

"I can handle it, Lieutenant. Not the first call I've been on."

"Quit with the attitude, Sharpe. I'm not like Brent. I won't be letting you off easy because you're gorgeous."

She gives me an icy stare as she pulls up to the call and gets out. I follow, expecting her to be just as bitchy with the people who called as she is with me. I'm a little surprised to see she's one hundred percent professional and handles the call with dignity and grace.

After she clears the call and pulls away from the scene, she looks at me. "Well, Lieutenant?"

"You stand too close to people. You want to be approachable but not put yourself in danger. If that had turned bad, you could've been in a fight and had no reaction time."

19

She huffs and says nothing. We take a few more calls before the radio chimes to life. "Squad Thirty-two."

She reaches for the mic on her shoulder. "Go ahead."

"Domestic dispute on Woodlawn Drive. Caller says her husband pushed her into a table and tried to break her wrist. No guns in the home, but he tried to stab her with a butcher's knife. Knife is no longer in the home. She said he chased her outside with it, and it got stuck in a tree when he attempted to use it on her."

I turn on the lights and sirens as Lyric responds. "Ten-four. En route." She steps on the gas and weaves her way perfectly in and out of traffic, but I can see the dark expression that crosses her face.

That fierceness.

Tenacity.

But there's something else. Something I can't quite place. It looks suspiciously like fear.

I take a chance. "You can never walk into these situations showing fear. Even if you are afraid, you need to tamp it down and work through it. Fear can put you just as much in a body bag as overconfidence can."

She shakes her head. "I'm fine."

I watch her closely, trying to decipher if she's telling the truth, as she pulls up to the call. She gets out and waits for me. We head up to the house together. I'm having a hard time letting her take the lead like I'm supposed to. Up until now, observing her on calls has been easy. But there's something about this one that's throwing me. Something about her reaction to it.

I knock hard on the door. "Gainesville Police! Open the door." We both listen. It's far too quiet. No one responds. "Gainesville Police!"

Lyric looks up at me, biting her lip. "She could be hurt," she says quietly.

I'm just about to pound on the door again when it opens. A frail woman who looks to be no more than eighteen answers the door. Her brown hair is snarled and matted. Her cheeks are tear-stained. She looks like she hasn't eaten in years and looks up at me with sunken, lifeless eyes.

"It's okay. I made a mistake."

A taller guy appears behind her. He has a piercing in his nose and lip. He's as skinny as she is, but has a look about him that sets me off. His

20

rainbow colored hair doesn't fool me. Neither does the unicorn on his shirt or his pink skinny jeans.

"What seems to be the issue, officers?"

It takes everything in me not to punch him. "We got a call of a disturbance," I say. "Just making sure it's all good."

"We argued. You know how it is. Got a little loud," he lies.

I look down at the woman. I can't see any bruises or marks on her, but she refuses to make eye contact with me or anyone else. I look back up at him. "Still need to check it out, sir."

"Really. Everything is okay," the woman says meekly. "I dropped a glass. It was his favorite. We got into an argument. We yelled at each other. I shoved him away. He shoved me back, but it's fine. There's nothing wrong."

"Thanks for the time, officers, but we're okay." The guy starts closing the door. I'm about to stop him, but Lyric steps in.

"Ms. Davidson? I'd like to speak with you in private please."

"Oh… No. It's okay. You guys can leave." Her eyes dart fearfully between the two of us. I shoot Lyric a look telling her to back off and let me deal with it, but she ignores me.

"Outside. Please." Lyric gives her a pleading look, then glares at me when the woman follows. She leads her to the side of the house, putting me and a little distance between them and the fucktard in front of me. He shoots daggers at them both as he folds his arms over his chest.

Their voices are low, but I can just make them out over my own questioning as I keep them both in my sights. Looking out for our partners is something we're all trained to do. But looking out for her is something I feel more of a pull to do. Something I can't explain, but I've never questioned myself.

"I'm really okay," the woman whispers.

"Ms. Davidson… Sometimes, it's difficult to trust that the police can help you when you're so afraid. You want to speak up, but you're hesitant. There are so many unknowns. You never know what he is going to do if you stay, or how he'll come after you if you leave. You're so scared to walk away because you fear you will always be looking over your shoulder wondering when, or if, he will strike. That he will find you and hurt you again. I understand that fear. I understand because I was you. I've been there. It's hard, and it's scary. Terrifying, really. But leaving was

21

the best thing I ever did. I packed up what little I had left and never looked back. My life is better for it. Now, it's your turn. You have to stand up for yourself because no one else will. You need to show that strength, that courage that I see inside you. Use that to walk away. To show him that he holds no power over you. He doesn't control you. He doesn't get to take that light that I see in you away. You need to be strong; to stand up and fight. If you don't, he wins."

"What if he comes after me?" she whispers.

He can't hear her as he talks to me, but with my trained ear, I can. I'm proud as fuck of Lyric and confused as hell. Her life is better for it? What the fuck does that mean?

Later, after we take the guy to prison, Lyric sighs heavily. I haven't been able to get my mind off what she said. Understanding the fear? She was in that position? I glance at her for the fiftieth time trying to figure out what the hell to say. Best thing she did was leave. The United Kingdom? Is that why she left without even finishing her training? What am I missing?

"What am I doing wrong now, Lieutenant?" she snaps.

I try to think of anything to broach the subject, but can't without sounding like a nosy fucking prick. Instead, I sigh. "You have to watch where you stand when you talk to people. I've said that before. You were standing so close to her that she could have grabbed your gun, and you wouldn't have known until it was too late and you were wrestling for it."

"I was trying to -"

I put a hand up to silence her. "I know. A rapport. But building a rapport and getting yourself killed are two different fucking things." I bite the inside of my cheek and turn to look out the window.

The rest of our day is filled with traffic stops with a disturbance or neighbor dispute thrown in. I give her as much feedback as I can, but the fact that she refuses to listen is annoying as all fuck. I tell her don't stand so close. She stands closer. I subtly give her cues to move back. She ignores them. She asks me to tell her what she's done wrong in the most mocking and insubordinate tone I've ever heard. Fuck. Why can't she just do what I say? Like her friend, Mariah.

She shoots me a glare as she pulls into the parking garage and parks. Without a word, she gets out and grabs her gear from the trunk. She storms into the building without a backwards glance. Fine with me. Maybe

22

I can get a damn grip on myself and figure out just what in the hell she meant with her comments on that domestic.

A few minutes later, as I'm packing up my gear to head home, finally, a shadow at my door forces me to look up. I catch my breath. Standing in front of me is Lyric. Her hair falling perfectly to her shoulders. Her bag is slung over her shoulder, almost engulfing her. Her purple tank top barely covers her luscious tits. Her blue jeans look like they may actually be painted on. My throat goes dry. I swallow. Hard. I can't take my eyes off her.

"You know, there's a way to tell someone that they're doing something incorrectly. I've almost completed eleven weeks of training. It isn't my fault that up until this point, everything I've done has been praised. I didn't know that the habits I'd made with standing closer to someone like I do is dangerous because I've never been told it's wrong. But you could tell me that. Nicely." She gives me a fierce look as she tosses her hair over her shoulder, and it pisses me right the fuck off.

"I spent the entire fucking day telling you to back up. I gave you signals to help you in your stance. You ignored all of them. I told you everything you need to improve on. You -"

"You didn't tell me to improve! You told me everything I was doing was wrong! Don't drive like that. You'll kill someone. Don't stand that way. They'll steal your gun. Don't talk that way. You're too timid. You're too sassy. Nothing I did was right for you!" She's flailing her arms and waving her hands wildly at me as she jabs the air. I can't decide if I'm pissed off or turned on. Probably both.

I glare at her just as dangerously as she is me. "All shit you need to fix! I mention a damn thing that you don't need to improve. You want to pass? Fix the problems and stop acting like a fucking know-it-all! Now, go home!"

Lyric winces slightly and cowers before she takes a deep breath to cover it. I don't think she realizes I saw it, but before I can apologize, she shoots searing fire from her eyes. She turns on her heel and disappears. I quickly round my desk and cross the room, but DJ appears in my doorway with Mariah.

Mariah looks up at me with her hands on her hips through narrowed eyes. "I can't believe you sometimes. I mean, I consider you a friend. One of my best. But for the love of fuck, you're so infuriating!"

Mariah and I became really close after her training. DJ is my best friend, but I might be closer to Mariah than I am to him.

I shake my head and look to DJ for an explanation. "Don't look at me. This is on you, man," DJ says unhelpfully. "I'm a little pissed that I spent the morning talking you up, and you turned around and were your typical asshole self."

"What? I was correcting -"

"No! You were being an asshole. You were acting the same way with her as you did with me when I first started here, and you got stuck training me," Mariah says, knocking me down a peg in true Mariah fashion. "You spent all day criticizing me. Not giving me any constructive feedback. You just told me everything I did wrong. Not how to fix it. You just did the same thing with her!"

I cross my arms over my chest. "Mariah, I'm not going to coddle her."

Mariah's blue eyes look like lightning bolts, and I find myself bracing for a hit. DJ steps in, though, and pushes her towards the direction Lyric went. "Go, baby. I'll handle him. Go find Lyric." Mariah listens, and I relax as she runs after her friend. DJ turns back to me. "Don't write her off, Matt. She has the potential to be one fuck of a cop. You've built this preconceived notion of her in your head that couldn't be further from the truth. Give her a chance. Work with her. You saw the same thing in Mariah that I do with Lyric." He glances down the hall before he looks back at me. He turns and walks after his girlfriend. "Fix it."

I growl low as I grab my gear and slam the door to my office behind me. I can see all of their points, but being put in my place by anyone, no matter how close I am to them, is not something I've ever swallowed well. It's like a bitter little pill that's stuck in my throat.

Truth is, I know I fucked up.

Only problem is...

I don't have a clue how to make it right.

24

Chapter Three

☆ Lyric ☆

(One Week Later)

I flip the pen in my fingers over and over again as I glare at the tall man at the front of the turnout room. His brown stubble and short brown hair compliments his coffee-colored eyes. The sleeve tattoos that run up both of his arms make me wonder how many more he hides underneath that dark blue dress shirt. The shirt that leaves nothing about his well-sculpted muscles to the imagination. Neither do those jeans. It's like his clothes were made just for him. Made to show him off like the amazing piece of art that he is.

Unfortunately, he's the biggest baboon's assface I've ever met. Well. Second biggest. He's so cocky and arrogant. He's such a jerk. He has no capability of being nice. He made up his mind about me before he even knew my name. I don't care what anyone says. Lieutenant Matt Chance is truly an asshole. He lives up to his reputation very well.

Tell that to my body, though. Every time he's in the same damn room, my entire world hums. It's impossible to hate him and stew over

25

what a dick he is when all I want to do is see if his cock is as big as his ego.

I growl low as I continue shooting a death glare at him. Fuck him. Fuck him for making me want to hate him. A man who looks as good as he does shouldn't be hated. He should be worshiped. All. Night. Long.

Who am I kidding? He probably is. If he doesn't have a wife or girlfriend, which seems unlikely, there's no way he can't get company for as long as he wants it. I'm sure he just has to look at her from across the bar with his steely gaze. The entire room, male and female, would fall at his feet and ask him how exactly they can please him.

I shake my head as Mariah sits next to me. "You know, it's really a shame. Matt is seriously stunning. But he's such a prick. Wrapped in a pretty package."

Mariah laughs. I look at her and sigh. Her blue eyes glitter with humor. "Matt has been through a lot of heartbreak."

I look at her incredulously. "What the hell does that have to do with him not being capable of being a decent human being?"

She smiles softly and squeezes my hand lightly. "He likes you, Lyric. I can tell. And so can DJ."

I'm taken aback. "No. I think you're missing something. Matt sure doesn't seem like he likes me."

"He doesn't have many friends, Lyric. He's been through…" She cuts herself off. "Just give him a chance."

"Listen up." Matt doesn't even have to raise his voice. He commands the entire room with just his tone. Everyone's eyes snap to him. His eyes meet mine for a moment. I look away, biting my lip. Matt waits a second while everyone quiets down. "We're still a trainer down. Brent is out on injury. I'll be on the streets today with Ms. Sharpe." A few groans can be heard. "Keep it up. Y'all will be directing traffic at the University just because I can. Next. Last night, patrol had a huge bust. One of the guys got away." He hands out a stack of papers. "I want this piece of shit in jail today. Last known location is on the back of the paper along with all known addresses."

"The bust was well over fifty-thousand dollars in heroin. I don't want that on my streets," DJ chips in as Matt continues handing out the papers. When he gets to the table Mariah and I are sitting at, he pauses. I

26

don't look up, but I can feel the scalding heat of his gaze, and I shiver. Fuck him for making me have any reaction to him.

I stare down at the picture of the guy we're looking for as Matt continues talking. I hate that his deep voice soothes me. And I need that. I'm so tired and on edge. The nightmares are nonstop. I've had one every night. The fire. Hamilton's face.

Tears sting my eyes, but I keep my head down and blink them away. I don't want Mariah to notice. She knows about the dreams. But I haven't told her about the phone calls I've been getting from unknown numbers. Nothing is ever said. Sometimes I can't even hear breathing. Just... silence.

It's unnerving. It happens at all hours of the day and night. I woke up this morning to my phone going off with yet another call. Same as before. Nothing. Just silence. Long silence from untraceable, unknown phone numbers. Just thinking about them makes my heart race out of control, and I subtly fight to keep myself from showing any signs of my discomfort. I love Mariah to death, but I don't want to reveal that.

Not yet.

The truth is, I don't know what to make of the calls. I know how many scams are going around. And I know how often a person picks up the phone, and no one answers. I have no reason to really think this could be anything more than that. I'm just getting in my head. I know I am.

Still... It's exhausting. And, if I'm being honest with myself, getting calls at three in the morning isn't a scam. I haven't heard of any telemarketer or scammer calling at that time of night... or morning, I guess.

I jump at Mariah's soft touch. She looks at me with questioning eyes. I shake my head. "I'm okay. Just... nightmares. I wake up and can't get back to sleep," I say softly as the turnout room clears out.

"Okay... Um..." She looks up at DJ briefly before she squeezes my arm and gets up. "Just... tell me if something else is going on?"

I smile as I stand and hug her briefly. "I promise."

She watches me a moment longer before turning and following DJ. I grab my gear and trail behind them, leaving Matt in the turnout room talking to the Captain. I'm far too tired to deal with him today.

The last week with him was almost insufferable. I nearly quit on more than one occasion. I couldn't do anything right. He picked apart

27

everything I did. Everything I said. He picked apart the way I stood. The way I drove. The way I stopped cars. Things I felt confident in, he found flaws. Today is the first day of my last week. What I should be excited about, I'm dreading. He's made me feel like I'm nowhere near ready to be on the streets on my own.

I run my hands up and down my arms. The air conditioning in this building never works right. It's either too hot or too cold. It's never the nice sixty-seven degrees they say it's set to. Today it feels like it's thirty degrees. My teeth are chattering. I have goosebumps. Maybe it's because I'm so tired. Sometimes, when I'm tired, I get really cold.

"Lyric. Wait up," the deep voice that sends warmth all through my body says from behind me. I close my eyes, continuing to hug myself, as I stop just before getting to the doors to the garage. I move to the wall just in case someone wants to get by.

I can smell him before I see him. His cologne is just as intoxicating as it is comforting. The spicy male scent that is Lieutenant Matt Chance is the most amazing smell I've ever had wrapped around me.

And I hate him more for it.

I open my eyes and look up at him, sensing he's moved in front of me. "Yes, Lieutenant?" My words are soft because speaking any louder would be more than I can take right now. Not only am I drained, but I'm experiencing everything that goes along with it. The nausea. The headache. The overpowering need to close my eyes and never open them, but being so hyper alert that closing them only succeeds in making my mind race with every detail of every tiny thing going on around me. Like the fly that just landed on the ceiling above me. I don't need to look to see it. I saw its shadow.

Matt looks down at me with something close to concern. But he's far too much of a jerk to ever do something like portray concern for anyone other than himself. "Lyric, are you okay?" He reaches up to tuck my hair behind my ear. For a moment I close my eyes and lean into his hand. Then I realize who he is and pull away.

"I'll be okay." I try to step around him and continue my journey to the garage. He gently grabs my arm.

"Hey, hang on."

I sigh and look up at him through my lashes, preparing for yet another ass chewing. "Yes, sir?"

28

Something crosses his eyes. Something… dark. Almost primal. He blinks, and it's gone. Something I probably imagined. "Listen, I just wanted to apologize. For last week. I was being an asshole, and I shouldn't have been. It's a defense mechanism with me. I…" He closes his eyes and scrubs both hands over his face as he opens them again. Fire. There's fire in the deep amber flecks he probably doesn't know he has. Fuck me for noticing.

"It's really okay, sir. I understand. I… have a lot of work to do if I want to be as good as you at this." I look down at his shoes. Why wouldn't his pristine black SWAT boots be as perfect as he is?

"No, Lyric. It isn't okay. I tore you down last week because I didn't want to be out there training new recruits. Mariah was the last one I trained. I became a Lieutenant right after, and there's a reason for that. I don't have the time I used to have to be training and patrolling and dealing with my duties with SWAT as well as my duties as a commanding officer. But none of that is an excuse to treat you the way I did. I'm sorry. This week will be better. I'll be constructive. Not just nitpick things and not tell you how to fix it. That's not my job. My job is to prepare you for what you're going to face on your own. Make you the best of the best."

I chew on my lip, not looking up at him, but immediately release it when I hear his low growl. He gently runs his thumb along my lip, leaving an inferno in its wake. I can't stop the shiver that runs directly between my legs and straight to the bundle of the nerves capable of making me shatter.

I squeeze my thighs together, hopefully not noticeably, before I smile softly up at him. "Okay. Forgiven." I squeeze his ridiculously muscular arm as I walk by him. More to ease my own need to touch him than for any other reason.

I hate my reaction to him. I'm not opposed to falling in love. But falling in love with him? I shake my head at myself as I put my gear in the trunk of the car. He puts his next to mine, brushing my hand, and I'm instantly shaky.

No.

He's my superior. Dating a superior officer. It's never a good idea. It's probably against department policy. We'd probably get fired and grow to resent each other. Or maybe it isn't. DJ is a Sergeant. He's with Mariah. They joke about keeping their relationship under wraps, but most everyone knows they're together.

29

I gently pull my hand back and begin my vehicle inspection. I can feel him watching me. I don't want him to stop, but the idea of just that sets me into a massive state of confusion.

Matt is… intolerable. He's impossible. It's his way or wrong. He's snappy. He lives up to his asshole reputation, then rockets past it to reach a level all his own. He's controlling. Dominant. Hot. He makes me all tingly and wet with just his timbre. And fuck if all that doesn't make me want him more.

Ugh! If I wasn't afraid he'd call me out for acting like a child, I'd stomp my foot. Fuck that. I'd jump up and down screaming like a banshee and throwing a tantrum to rival a toddler who threw her dummy into a mud puddle.

"Ready to head out, rookie?" Matt asks with a stupidly charming smile.

I fight back a pout. "Yes, Lieutenant." I look at him briefly, giving him another soft smile. He turns away quickly and ducks into the squad. What is wrong with me? How can I go from envisioning his demise in my head not fifteen minutes ago to envisioning what it would be like to ride him; his, what I'm fairly certain is large, cock buried so deep inside me he'll never get out?

Ridiculous. I'm being ridiculous.

That doesn't stop me from creating very dirty fantasies in my mind the entire day. He praised my traffic stop technique. Said I learned a lot over the week and is proud of me. I started thinking of him rewarding me by bending me over the squad car as my nails dug into the hood while he gave me the hardest, fastest fuck of my life.

He opened the door for me at lunch. I started looking for a bathroom because all I could think about was him slamming me against the wall and claiming me. Over and over again while I tugged his hair and screamed his name.

I refuse to take it further than thoughts. I'm terrified for so many reasons. I only went on one date with Hamilton. One. And dealt with months of torture. Him not leaving me alone. Trying to force me to go on another date with him. Angry when I refused. Stalking me. Burning down my house. Taking everything from me. The attack… No one but Tyler knows about that. Not even Mariah.

30

I need to go home. The looks he gives me when he doesn't think I notice are playing with my mind. The compliments. Soft touches. His deliberate attempts at making me laugh when he thinks I'm being too quiet. It's too much. I can't... I can't handle it. Thank God, thank everything, that the day is ending. Because being around him anymore is far too much for me.

If I let it, my heart would fall so far for him. So fast. But I won't. I can't. I know what obsession does. I won't ever let myself be put into that position again. Even though I know with everything I am that it wouldn't be like that with him, that little nagging voice puts so many doubts in my mind. Fuck Hamilton for making me a hesitant little girl. Fuck him for still having that control over me.

Maybe I should jump in. Head first. Maybe I should take control over my heart and run with it. Straight into the arms of Matt. I glance at Matt as I park the car. His eyes snap to the wall in front of us. I don't understand why he keeps doing that. He's never been shy before. Now he's acting all... un-Matt-like. It's... something that throws me. I don't know what to make of it

I have to get home. I need to regroup and get my head on right. I can't think. My mind is all over the place. One side thinks Matt might actually like me. Then the other thinks I'm being completely crazy. Then the two collide into this explosion of insanity, and I feel like the idea of getting into a relationship when I'm unaware of where the hell my stalker could be hiding is pure madness.

I beeline for the locker room, forgetting my gear in the trunk and ignoring Matt calling me. I just need to get somewhere. A place I can breathe. I can't get enough oxygen with his incredible scent filling me. I need distance. Just enough to... think. I need to just think.

"Lyric!" Matt nearly growls as he grabs my arm. I almost go limp. I stop breathing. I'm too scared to fight. Images of Hamilton flash through my mind, but I don't know why.

He's not here. Lyric! Calm down. It's Matt. Not Hamilton... I force my eyes to his, focusing on those sexy amber flecks. If I look hard enough, I can see myself in his eyes. And he's not looking at me with hatred. It's not like Hamilton. His eyes are a tornado of flames. They look like he could combust, and I don't know what's happening.

31

Matt backs me against a wall and crushes his lips to mine, devouring my mouth with his. Hungry. His tongue forces its way in to meet mine. Clashing. Scorching it with his need. My fingers grip his belt while the other hand spears his hair. I moan, sucking on his tongue.

He bites my lip while his hands destroy any last resolve I have at staying away from him. His body molds itself to mine. I can feel every ridge; every sharp edge. His leg slips between my thighs, and my body responds on its own. I rub myself against him, relieving the pressure he's built up all day.

"Fuck, Lyric, you taste like every sinful fantasy I've ever had," he says against my lips. He kisses his way down to my neck.

"Matt… Oh God," I pant as I tilt my head to give him more access. His fingers dig into my ass as he pulls me closer to him. Somehow through my delirium and glazed over eyes, I see DJ and Mariah walk through the door that leads to the garage. They step into the hall. DJ turns quickly, keeping Mariah from seeing what's happening, and I'm suddenly crashing back to reality. I push back against him as he bites my neck. "Matt… no. Stop!"

Panic nearly stops my heart, but I don't know why. I know I'm not in danger. I know Matt would never hurt me. But I can't think. I need to. I can't breathe. I feel the tears sting my eyes, but Matt still has his arms around me. He's too close. I shake my head as I wiggle free, ignoring the look of pure concern and slight fear in his eyes.

"Lyric?" he asks, shaking his head like he's coming out of his own haze.

"No!" I shove him harder back as images of Hamilton crowd my mind. "No… no!"

"Lyric, what's happening?"

I try focusing on his voice, but it's not enough. Everything I worked so hard to forget slams into me with the force of ten atomic bombs, the likes of the one dropped on Hiroshima. I can't feel my heartbeat anymore. All I can feel is Hamilton. His slimy hands around my throat. His hot, disgusting onion and garlic breath in my face.

I run.

I run because I have no other choice.

I have to get away.

I have to get away from him.

32

He'll kill me if I don't.

Chapter Four

☆ Matt ☆

"What the fuck? Lyric!" I watch as she flees down the hall towards the locker room. I instantaneously turn to chase her, but I'm pulled back. Hard. Mariah flies down the hall as DJ holds me back. I yank my arm free, but he shoves me against the wall I just had Lyric against. "What the hell are you doing? Let go!" I try to shove him off me, but he shoves me back harder.

"Stop! Listen to me for a fucking second!" We both turn as other officers start moving into the hall from the garage. DJ backs off and gives me a look to follow him. He quickly walks down the hall, past the locker room. I hesitate, fighting myself on going in there and trying to figure out what made her eyes shoot open in terror.

"What the hell happened, DJ?"

"Not here." He strides quickly to my office as I shoot daggers at his back. He moves aside when we get there and closes the door behind us.

"I don't know what the fuck just happened, but she just looked right through me. Like she didn't hear a word I said. She didn't even see me, DJ."

"Look. Matt, that girl has been through far more than you or I could ever imagine."

I feel like I've been sucker punched in the nuts. Her comments last week at the domestic call flood back to me. "Like what?"

"Like shit I don't know. Shit she hasn't even told Mariah. But we can tell. We know there's things she hasn't opened up about. Things she's not ready to open up about. But as for your question about what just happened? What you just saw out there?" He points in the direction of the garage. "That should tell you that whatever the fuck happened to that girl is something really fucking serious."

I groan and run my hands over my face. "I shouldn't have kissed her like that. All fucking day all I could think about was her in my bed. I jumped on her like a starving wolf." I shake my head. "I'd be terrified of me, too. I should've listened to my damn self and stayed the hell away from her."

"That's not the answer."

"DJ, my tastes are…" I don't really know how to tell him everything, but I know I need to. Especially if I expect him to help me with Lyric. I haven't wanted a relationship in a long time because of what happened with my last one. I haven't really even wanted to allow my dominant bedroom manner out, but it's hard to tamp that shit. I sink in my chair and look up at him.

"I know what you do in your spare time, Matt. We've been friends a long time."

I shake my head. "You don't know why. I've only told one person what happened. Why I can't allow myself to be in a relationship again."

DJ raises an eyebrow and sits. "I always thought it was because you hadn't found anyone to settle with."

I slowly shake my head. "It's because I almost killed the woman I was dating."

DJ nearly chokes.

I hold up a hand to stop him from talking. "It's not like that. I was with her one night. Things got hot and heavy. We were having sex. I choked her. I didn't realize I was doing it. I'd done it before. She asked me to. It wasn't anything new. But I lost control. I wasn't paying attention to her signs. I was too busy paying attention to how good she felt. Next thing I know, she was passed out. I thought she was dead."

35

"Fuck."

"I haven't been in a relationship since. And there's a very large part of me that I'm terrified to let out. Yeah, I have kinks. I like the control. I like my cuffs and ties. But…" I shake my head and close my eyes a second before opening them again.

"But you're afraid you're going to lose control. That's why you hit the clubs and find particular types of women who are into your type of kinks."

I shrug. "I needed to practice keeping the control. Fuck. I needed the control. And I'm good at keeping it. There's particular things I don't do anymore. Choking is one of them. No matter how much she begs for it. The problem? I can see the submissive in Lyric. And she's fucking calling to me. The dominant in me. The dominant that I've fought for years to keep at bay."

DJ stands. "I'm a dominant, Matt. And I can tell you better than anyone that as soon as you find your submissive, there's no turning back. She's not going away. It's obvious that she's just as meant for you as Mariah is for me. You won't be able to fight that. And you shouldn't. You fucked up. Learned. Time to move on from it."

"Did you forget she fucking ran from me? Lyric doesn't want anything to do with my dominant side either. I lost complete control out there. I don't like that she can make me do that. She could get hurt."

"Stop it. That's not true at all. You know it. You think I don't lose control?" He looks towards the door when he hears voices. I don't miss that one of them is Lyric. I also don't miss the sniffle. DJ looks back at me. "Don't let your past get in the way of what you could have with her. Lyric is an amazing woman. She compliments you. I've seen it. Mariah has seen it. Fuck, I've known for longer than you probably think I have that you're meant for each other. But she's been through some shit. Don't give up on her." He heads for the door, but turns just before he opens it. "Or on you."

I watch as he walks out the door, closing it behind him. I catch a glimpse of Lyric behind him. Her tear-stained cheeks are evident, but that fear in her eyes I saw earlier has been replaced with something else. I only needed a second to see her to know it's a deep rooted sadness. I'm not sure what put it there or who, but I'll gladly spend every second of the rest of my life fixing it.

36

Because DJ is right. I can't give up on her any more than I can on myself. I've given up on myself for a long time. Not because I wanted to. But because I hadn't found anyone I wanted to spend more than a night with. I hadn't found anyone who made me feel a fraction of what Lyric does.

Now, I need to figure out how to make her trust me and realize that despite what fucked up past we came from, all that matters is the moment we're in. And fuck if I don't want her in all of them.

(Two Weeks Later)

It's been almost two weeks since the night I kissed Lyric when we got back to headquarters. I still don't know what happened, but I can tell she's starting to trust me more. She's opening up. Being more... real. More herself.

I took DJ's advice for the both of us. I'm not giving up. When I allowed myself to admit the truth, I knew I wouldn't be able to give up on her or a future with her if I tried. Since that kiss, she's managed to burrow herself deep within me. No way I could get her out. I wouldn't want to. She's too deep. I'm too deep.

I look down at Lyric snuggled into my side as the movie we were watching ends. I don't really know what was playing. Most of my night has been spent thinking of how soft her body feels next to me. How incredible she feels. Like she's cut from my side and is meant to be there. Like she's mine.

She looks up at me with adorably wide eyes and blinks a few times. I zero in on her full lips, wanting to kiss her but not sure if I dare. Seeing her run from me the way she did was something I don't ever want to see again. I decided I'd do this at her pace. If she wants a kiss, she'll have to be the one to take it.

Lyric surprises me when she shifts with a soft smile and leans in like she's going in for that kiss, but the shrill beat of a song I've never heard cuts through the air. Lyric jumps and grips my shirt a moment before sighing and turning away.

37

But not before I see it.

Fear.

She picks up her phone and takes a deep breath before answering. "Hello?" She bites her lip and looks down at her hands as she clears her throat and listens for a moment. "Hello." It's nearly a whisper, and I become concerned rather quickly.

I give her a look as I lean in close to her trying to hear. "Who is it?" I ask quietly.

She sniffles and lets out a muffled sob before hanging up and shaking her head as she stands. I watch her, growing increasingly more troubled as the seconds tick by. "No one." She nearly darts to the bathroom.

"Lyric!" I growl. She stops dead in her tracks and looks at me submissively. Fucking hell. I stand and walk to her. "Who the fuck was that? Don't shut me out again." I use a very stern and commanding voice. The voice that's always gotten people to do exactly as I say when I say it.

Lyric looks down. "Please. Don't make me." I can hear the tears in her voice as she wraps her arms around herself.

I tuck a strand of hair behind her ear, stepping closer but refusing to pull her in my arms. I don't want her to run again. "Tell me. Now, Lyric. This has gone on long enough. I deserve to know what the hell is happening."

She sniffles, whispering softly, "It's… my stalker. From… the United Kingdom."

It feels like a fist is clenching my heart. "Your… stalker?" I'm trying to understand the words, but all I can think of is that she's in danger. Every protective cell in my body stands at immediate attention ready to fight.

She slowly nods. "He… lives in the UK. Where I'm from…" She takes a deep breath and starts trembling. I can't hold back. I crush her into my chest. She jumps a little and flinches, instinctively trying to pull back, but I don't let her. I'm done with all of that. I need her close to me, and I know she needs to feel me. To feel safe.

"Lyric, please. Please tell me," I whisper into her hair as I hold her tightly and sway with her. Vanilla bean. Unique to her. I've never smelled anything like her. She's fresh. She's sweet. She's everything I've already decided I need in my life.

After a few moments, she takes a deep breath. "He asked me out. We went on one date. No more. He… got… really obsessed with me. He… wouldn't leave me alone. He started staying after his shift until I got there for mine. And he showed up early for his so he was there when I left for the night. I caught him following me a few times. One day… he… was really upset. I didn't show up for a date he demanded I went to. I went for a drive… after work… and…" She bursts into a fresh wave of sobs, gripping the waistband of my jeans as she tries to catch her breath.

I keep swaying with her, running my fingers through her hair. "I got you. I'm right here."

"He… set my house… on fire!" She trembles. "He took everything from me just because I wouldn't date him!"

"Jesus…" I kiss the side of her head, then her neck. My grip on her tightens. She holds onto me for dear life, but says nothing more. I don't want to upset her, but I need to know. "What about what you said at the domestic?"

She looks up at me in surprise. "You… heard what I said?"

"It's my job to be in tune to what my trainees and my partners are doing and saying. It's part of the reason the department hates that I don't want to train anymore. I'm really good at it."

She smiles softly and hides back in my chest. "When I was waiting for my Visa to get approved, I was living with my trainer from the department I worked with. I was… am… rather close with him. He… was… is… like a father to me. I was forced to quit the department because, at first, the department wouldn't do anything about him. But when the evidence was combed through, it was found out that he really did set my house on fire. He…"

I can sense how hard it is for her to continue. She digs her nails into my waistband so tightly, I'm fairly convinced if she lets go, she'll fade into nothingness.

"Lyric, I promise I'm here for you, pretty girl. I'm not going anywhere. You can trust me. I won't let anything happen to you." I whisper the words in her ear and let her hold me as tightly as she damn well pleases. I'd give her the world if she asked me for it. I wouldn't be able to deny her anything.

"One day when Tyler left for work, my stalker showed up at the house. He… beat me… so badly that…" I can feel her bite my shirt as she tries to steady herself. "I… couldn't move. He threw me into walls and… tables. He hit me. Slapped me. I… c-couldn't fight b-back." She's shaking her head as her tears soak my shirt. If I wasn't holding her up, she'd be curled in a ball on the floor. My fingers grip the back of her shirt to steady myself. I need to be strong for her, but all I want to do right now is tear the world apart.

"Fuck, baby." I can't do anything but run my fingers through her hair and keep my lips pressed to her ear as I hug her.

"I… had… to live in a safehouse… until I could leave the c-c-country!" She's starting to hyperventilate.

I hug her tighter and kiss her head, cheek, neck, and forehead. I keep running my fingers through her hair doing anything I can think of to soothe her.

"Hamilton disappeared. We… h-haven't heard from him. He… comes from a wealthy family and they helped him avoid prosecution. For the fire and… everything he did to me." She's whispering, but at least she's not hyperventilating.

"And now he's calling?"

She nods. "He knows. He knows I'm here." She pulls away. I reluctantly let her because I don't want to scare her, but I watch her closely. She hugs herself again as her eyes dart wildly around the room. Before I can say much of anything, she turns and almost runs to her bedroom.

"Honey, what are you doing?"

"I have to get out of here. He knows where I am. I have to move. It's the only way." She starts pulling things out of her closet and throwing them in a pile on the floor. "I don't have a choice." I can hear the misery in her voice, but it's overpowered by the pounding of my heart.

"Wait. What?" I try to follow her logic while attempting to calm myself down and think logically. "Move?"

"There's no other option. He knows where I am."

"Lyric. Wait. Stop." I grab her arm, but she yanks it free and continues pulling everything out of her closet. I grab both of her arms and haul her back against my chest wrapping my arms around her chest to keep her from moving.

"Let go! What are you doing? Don't you understand? He's found me! I have to go!"

40

"No. No. I'm not letting you go. Not after how far we've come over the last couple weeks. I'm not going to fucking lose you, Lyric. Let me help you. I can keep you safe." The idea of her walking out of my life isn't something I can handle. I'd never come back from it.

"I can take care of myself! I've done it for a year!" She's getting hysterical as she flails against me in an effort to free herself. I only tighten my grip in response.

"I don't doubt you can take care of yourself, but you don't have to. You're not alone. You have me now."

"And be some damsel in distress? A fucking princess with glitter hair, and a pink dress? In need of a prince to come and save her? Fuck you! No! Let me go! I can handle it on my own!"

"Is that what you want? To fucking leave when I can tell you feel something for me? I fucking know it's just as strong as the way I feel for you. You're not going anywhere! I'm not letting it happen!"

She manages to spin herself around in my arms and level me with a glare that could melt titanium. But there's more behind it. Passion. An explosion of it. "You don't get to tell me what to do."

"And you don't get to just leave." I growl the words as I lean down and take what's mine. Her mouth immediately submits to mine. Instead of pushing against my chest, she's gripping my shirt in her tiny hands. She whimpers into my mouth as my tongue finds hers and begins a sexy rumba.

"Matt," she breathes.

"I won't let you go. You're mine, Lyric. Do you understand?"

She nods and wraps her arms around my shoulders, pressing herself against me. Her hardened nipples against my chest make my body sing for her. "I don't want anyone else. Is that stupid? After what I just went through? Being claimed by a man I didn't want?"

She looks at me with so much confusion, I don't know how to respond with words. Instead, I shake my head and kiss her again. Long and deep. Her body molds to mine. She starts to lift my shirt, but hesitates. I pull back long enough to take it off and tug hers off, too. Her tits spill out for me. I'd forgotten she wasn't wearing a bra. That as soon as we got here today, the first thing she did was change into a tight as fuck tank top and sexy as hell shorts that show off just a hint of her ass cheeks.

"Fuck me, you're beautiful."

41

Her cheeks turn a pretty shade of pink, and she looks down. Her fingertips are tucked in the waistband of my jeans. "I am not. I'm... average."

I smile and reach down, gripping her thighs as I lift her. Her eyes widen as she wraps her legs around my waist. My lips crash to hers again and again on my way to the bed. I can feel how much she wants me.

This.

I feel it in her touch. I can see it in the way she's looking at me right now. An unadulterated desire. Hunger. A need to devour me as much as I need to consume her.

"Fucking beautiful." I drop her on the bed watching her bounce gently, her tits moving with the subtle bobbing of her body. I drink her in as I take a deep breath. I have to know she's okay with this. "Lyric, I..." I've never been so nervous asking a fucking question.

"I want this. I do." She looks me square in the eye, mirroring all of the heat building inside me, and it's all the permission I need. "I need to feel safe and protected. Claimed. I just need to feel something more than fear."

I tug her shorts down, tossing them somewhere as I unbutton my jeans. I kick out of them and scramble on top of her like a too eager teenager having sex for the first time. Usually my tongue would be buried in her smooth as silk pussy, but my dick has other plans. I've wanted her for months. Waiting is impossible.

As soon as my tip makes its way inside, and I feel how tight she is, I realize that my plan to sink myself inside her and never leave her warmth and wetness is shot to hell. She's as tight as a virgin. I question if she is, and immediately look down at her with worry.

"Are... Have.... you never...?" My dick twitches. Her hips jerk in response, and she bites her lip. She looks down at my chest. Her cheeks darken as she nods. "Jesus fuck." I'm suddenly shaky and nervous. I don't want to hurt her. I'm fully aware I'm far larger than average. I'll tear her pussy apart if I don't watch myself.

"I..." She looks up at me through her lashes. "Does that change... anything?"

I shake my head slowly. "Just the pace." I slowly slide a little further into her, closing my eyes and groaning when she tightens around me. I wait for her to relax before giving her more. Inch by inch. Second by agonizing second.

Finally, I'm nestled so deeply inside her, and she's looking up at me with such intensely trusting eyes, that I nearly start weeping like a five-year-old girl. I lean down to kiss her, more to compose myself than the need I have to taste her peach flavored lip gloss. She wraps her arms as tightly around my shoulders as her legs are around my waist, and her pussy is around my dick.

Slowly and as gently as I possibly can, I start moving, thrusting inside her with all the tenderness I possess. She meets each slow and deliberate thrust with a soft sigh and moan as she kisses my neck. Her nails dig into my back when I start kissing my way down to her luscious tits as I thrust a little faster. Harder. Deeper.

"Matt…," she whispers as her fingers spear my hair. I lick her nipples in turn before letting my teeth scrape lightly across each one. I leave sweet kisses along her collarbone. Her neckline. Her jaw. When I reach her lips, she throws her head back with a groan. Her pussy tightens around me, and I shift, pushing my dick against the same spot that just drove her nearly over the edge.

"Fuck, baby. You don't know how good you feel."

Her eyes glaze over as she nips at my lower lip. I kiss her long and hard, dominating her lips with mine. I let my hand make its way softly down her body, leaving goosebumps in its wake, until I reach her pussy. As I thrust deeply inside her, I start rubbing her most sensitive bundle of nerves.

"Oh… Fuck! Matt!" she screams. Her body jerks against mine, and her pussy clenches and pulses so deliciously around my dick, that I nearly come. She pants as I look down at her, increasing the hardness of my thrusts and quickening the pace that my thumb is rubbing her clit. She jerks against me again and looks at me so sweetly. "Please…" She bites her lip as she whispers the plea. I'm a fucking goner. She has no idea what her naturally submissive nature does to me.

My dick jerks inside her tight pussy, begging me for release. I lean down and kiss her softly as I pinch her clit. "Come for me, my pretty girl."

She shatters. She screams and comes so hard she rips my own release from me. "Matt! Oh, fuck yes!"

43

"Lyric! Holy God, baby girl." I grip her almost as hard as she is me as our bodies rock against each other. I spill everything into her, and she greedily sucks it all up. Her pussy grips my dick with each and every pulse as we both come.

After several very long moments with my dick still buried deeply inside her, I flip us both so she's on top of me. She makes the cutest moaning noises as her hair spills over my shoulder and she cuddles into my chest. She spreads her legs wider pushing me deeper inside her, and it's my turn to moan. She kisses my neck as I tuck the blanket around us.

"I'm so stupidly in love with you," she whispers. "Is that wrong?"

I wrap my arms around her and kiss her forehead as I tangle my fingers in her hair. "No. Because I'm so fucking in love with you, too."

"Mmm…" I feel her breathing even out. Moments later, I can tell she's asleep.

I've never made love to a woman. I've never in my life found a woman I wanted to make love to. After sharing this moment with her, I know that she's the only one I'll ever do this with. I don't want anyone else but her.

She's mine.

And I won't let any fucked up, obsessed, rich, pretty boy, motherfucking, thinks-he-can-have-whatever-the-fuck-he-wants asshole take what's *mine*.

44

Chapter Five

☆ Lyric ☆

I blink sleepily awake to the far away sound of... something. Through the haze and blur, I vaguely make out Matt reaching for something. I bite my lip at thoughts of the night before. I love that he was so gentle with me. Even though I could sense with every part of me that he didn't want to be.

I love that he made last night so special for me, being that it was my first time. As embarrassing as that is to admit. Twenty-nine and never had sex. Not to say that I haven't explored things on myself. I know what I like. I've just never found anyone that I trust enough to give myself to in that way.

Until Matt.

I look at him shyly as he shakes the haze away and answers his phone groggily. "Hello?" The raspiness of his voice is one of the sexiest things about him. But in the morning... I blush at the thoughts running through my mind. But heat pools between my thighs anyway.

Matt lays back on his back and holds out an arm. "Mmm..." I waste no time curling into his side. I kiss his chest as he kisses my forehead and hugs me. I drop my arm low around his waist, shyly letting my forearm rest just above his dick.

Matt holds the phone away from his ear and looks at it a moment before bringing it back to his ear. "Hello?" He's quiet for a moment, but I can feel him tense. "Listen. I know who the fuck you are. You may as well just tell me where you are, so I don't need to go hunting." The growl into the phone rumbles in his chest.

My eyes widen. I look up at him. "It... can't be..."

He slowly sits up. "Fucking breathing into the phone isn't helping you. Scared that you're talking to a man instead of a woman you feel like you can intimidate?"

I back slowly away and curl into myself at the edge of the bed as I watch him get more tense as the seconds go by. "No..." I don't know why I find myself in a state of disbelief right now. Maybe it's because ten seconds ago I felt safe. Secure. More than I have since I left the United Kingdom.

"You what?" he asks dangerously. Darkly. I close my eyes. "Why don't you come over here? I'll show you exactly what you'll face when you meet me. See how it feels when you come up against someone who pushes back." I open my eyes and watch as Matt stands. "Tell me where you are, you fucker!" His voice is getting less dangerous and more erratic. Out of control. Loud... "Tell me where the fuck you are!" I cover my ears and burrow under the covers with just my eyes peeking out. "Tell me where the fuck you are, you fucking asshole!" He stops at my closet and punches the wall. I flinch and squeeze my eyes closed. "Fuck!"

"Ah!" I scream as something shatters against the wall. I don't know what. I didn't see it. I cover my head with the blanket and tremble under the covers like a child.

"Lyric?"

I burrow and shake uncontrollably as I wipe my eyes, feeling slightly idiotic. "I'm fine. I'm sorry. I'm fine."

Matt crawls under the covers and wraps me in his strong arms. My nails dig shakily, but gently into his chest as I press myself as closely against him as I can possibly get. I breathe in his cologne and let it work its magic. I don't know how it happens, but it calms me.

He calms me.

46

His fingers run soothingly through my hair as he kisses the side of my head. "I'm sorry. I didn't mean to scare you. I'll buy you a new phone."

I shake my head, confused. "What?"

"That was your phone that shattered against the wall. I'll buy you a new one." He hugs me tighter.

I sink into his embrace. "What did he say?"

"It doesn't matter. It's never going to happen."

I look up at him. Part of me wants to argue. Tell him I can handle it. I've been handling it for the past couple years or however long it's been now. But the other part of me likes that I don't have to. I like that he's willing to shield me from it. I've spent so many years trying to be tough and independent. Trying to take care of everything on my own just to prove to everyone, to myself, that I could. That I can.

But looking into Matt's protective eyes right now... "I don't want to be the strong one anymore. I'm tired of it. I just want someone to take care of me for once. Is that wrong?"

"No, Lyric. It's not. I know how strong you are. I know you want the world to see it. To see you the way I do. But you don't have to be that fierce woman standing tall in the face of a fucking hurricane anymore. At least not on your own. You have me to lean on now. To be that barrier between you and the storm." He tugs my hair and leans down to kiss me.

I close my eyes and melt into the kiss with a whimper. When he pulls away, I'm dazed. I slowly open my eyes and take a deep breath. "I... don't want to be that girl that hides behind her man for every little thing. But... I..." I trail off trying to think of the right words.

"But... you don't want to fight alone anymore."

I nod, a little curious about how he knows what I'm trying to say better than I do. "Does that make me weak?"

"Baby, asking for help? Come on. Asking for help shows just how fucking strong you are."

"I hate how weak he makes me feel..."

"Weak? Lyric, you're one of the strongest women I know. You're loyal. You're devoted and kind. But you're also tough. You're feisty. Sassy. I love how inquisitive you are. You're brave. I can list a hundred more things about you. Weak isn't one of them."

"Crazy?"

"Honest."

"Meek?"

"Fearless."

"Stubborn?"

"Definitely stubborn. One of the most infuriatingly stubborn women I've ever met."

I feel my cheeks heat up, and I hide in his chest as I giggle quietly. "You really think all of that about me?"

"Yes. I also think you're stunningly beautiful. You consistently find new ways to take my breath away." He runs one hand up my body, cupping my tit on the way and making me gasp, before he reaches my chin. He tilts my face up so my eyes meet his. "We'll get through this. You're not alone. Okay? Not this time."

"I understand." My eyes travel to his full, kissable lips. All I can think about right now is them on mine. I don't want to think about Hamilton. I don't want to think about my past. I don't want to think about the calls.

Reading me like a book, which I'm quickly starting to love, Matt leans down and presses his lips to mine. He deepens the kiss, slipping his tongue between my lips, tangling it with mine. I melt against him, concentrating on nothing but the way he feels against me; the goosebumps I get when he softly trails his fingertips along my skin.

We both jump slightly when his phone chimes. He groans. "I have a meeting today. I can't be late. Brody may actually kill me this time if I walk into another meeting after it started."

I slightly deflate. I don't want him to stop, but I also don't want him to get into trouble. "I understand…," I say softly.

He cups my cheek in his palm, and I lean into it. "Be my good girl, and I promise I'll make it up to you." He leans down to kiss me.

It feels like a bolt of electricity shoots right to my center when his lips meet mine. I close my eyes and whine quietly when he pulls away and starts to get up. I instantly miss his warmth, but watching his cocky strut while he makes his way to the bathroom is enough to have me biting my lip and rubbing my thighs together.

Resigned to the conclusion I'm not going to get more of the magic he gifted me last night, I get up. I sneak into the bathroom and quietly clean up, not wanting to interrupt his shower. I can't help sneaking glances at his perfect silhouette hidden behind the steam on the shower's glass door. I fight myself to wipe the steam off and catch a glimpse of his perfectly chiseled body through the glass.

Before I can act on all of the dirty fantasies he puts in my head, I quickly and silently run out of the bathroom. I get dressed and head out to the kitchen trying to put distance between the two of us, but I find myself smiling softly and humming a tune I've never heard as thoughts of last night slip into my mind.

I absently suck some waffle batter off my thumb with a shy smile thinking of his hands caressing my body. It was like I was an instrument that only he knew how to play. Like I was a singer whose voice only sang for him. Like my body is ablaze and craves him.

I jump slightly when I feel his hands on my hips and lips on my neck. He wraps his arms around me and sways with me as he watches me pull the waffles out of the waffle maker. Everything about him, everything he does and says, makes me feel like I'm the only person in the world.

"How do you feel? After last night?" he whispers in my ear before he kisses just below it, sending shockwaves throughout my whole body.

"Really good," I whisper shyly, my cheeks flushing.

He kisses my neck. "Go finish getting ready, honey. I'll finish this."

Matt surprises me by gently guiding me towards the bedroom. He swats my ass, and I giggle like a schoolgirl as I run into my room. I don't know how he does it, but as I finish getting ready I have to squeeze my thighs together to keep myself from begging him to relieve the pressure. Now that I've tasted him, I can't get enough.

"Ready for this, beautiful?" Matt asks as he pulls into his assigned parking space in the department's garage.

I tilt my head in confusion as I look at him. "Ready for what?"

He chuckles as he gets out of his ridiculously gigantic black Ford F-150 truck. He reaches in the back and grabs both of our gym bags filled with our police gear. I jump down and meet him at the back. He holds out a hand. "Shit's about to get real."

49

"You're scaring me a little bit here."

"Not trying to. Just fair warning. I have a reputation. You know it better than anyone. People are going to know soon enough that we're together. It's going to become a shit show of relentless teasing. For both of us."

I take his hand with a sigh. "I still don't completely understand."

He leads me into the building. "You know what people think of me. I'm a complete asshole. I'm tough. I'm insufferable. Well, those are all the same reasons why everyone we work with thinks I don't have a wife or girlfriend, even though I'm almost forty. People are going to be shocked when they realize that I'm with you. Not because of who you are. But because of who I am. They are going to tease you relentlessly because you're dating such a jerk. Think you can handle that?"

I pretend to think about the implications he's suggesting just to make him sweat a little. The truth is I don't care how much any of our colleagues tease us. I see exactly how much Mariah gets teased about DJ. How she just gives it right back to everyone. But the concerned look on Matt's face right now as he looks down at me is far too adorable to ignore.

"I don't know… That's…" I look down at our hands with the saddest look I can manage. I bite my tongue to keep from laughing.

Matt stops and looks down at me. "Hey. I won't let it get too bad. It's harmless bullshit, but it gets out of hand, I'll deal with it. You know that. At least you should by now."

I look up at him but can't hold back the laugh. "The look on your face!" I laugh harder as I tug him through the doors on my way to the locker room.

"Did you just…? Fuck, you scared me."

"I couldn't help it. Your concern was adorable. It really was."

"Adorable? I'm not adorable. Sexy. Hot. Super fucking controlling. Not adorable."

I glance back at him. "Adorable." I turn for the locker room, but Matt obviously has other ideas. I nearly trip when his grip on my hand tightens, and he pulls me through the cubicles to his office. He closes the door behind us and doesn't bother turning the light on. Although the shade is drawn, there's enough sunlight coming in to lighten the room enough for both of us to see each other.

Matt pushes me against the wall, kissing me hard and deeply. I whimper and moan at the same time, spearing his hair with my fingers and tugging lightly as his tongue finds its way into my mouth. He grabs my wrists and moves them both over my head. He holds them both against the wall with one of his large hands.

The other trails down my body. He squeezes both of my tits as he continues to kiss me, swallowing my moans and sighs of pleasure. My body arches into him. I can't control it. I don't want to.

His thumb flicks open the button on my pants, and before I know what's happening, his hand is slipping into my panties. He cups my pussy and holds me firmly against the wall with his body as my knees buckle at his touch.

He kisses down my neck with low, sexy growls that send vibrations directly to my pussy. He nips my neck as one of his deliciously long fingers thrusts hard into me. I bite his shoulder to cover my moans as I grip his hands, anything I can grip being that I'm pinned, to keep from falling.

"Mmm!"

"Ssh, baby." He gives me long, hard, fast, and deep thrusts flicking my clit with his thumb at the same rapid pace his finger is fucking me. It takes only seconds before my thighs start shaking and my pussy clenches around his finger. He pulls out slowly as he kisses up my jaw to my lips. He kisses me deeply before he pulls totally away. He brings his finger to his mouth and sucks me off it with a cocky smirk.

I look at him with hooded eyes, slowly coming out of a daze. I shake my head as I realize what he just did. "Why… did you stop?"

"Maybe next time you'll think twice before you make me think you're upset about something only to turn around and tell me you're teasing me."

My mouth drops. "I… really was only teasing."

"And it upset me thinking you might be upset." He reaches down and buttons my pants as he leans down to kiss me. I close my eyes, reveling in his familiar taste mixed with the sweet and tangy taste of myself on his tongue. "Next time you decide to tease me, make sure it's about something funny. Your happiness and other people fucking with it isn't something I will ever take lightly. Understand?"

51

I nod, suddenly feeling sick to my stomach at the thought that I upset him in any manner at all. All I want to do is please him. A strange feeling, since I've never really cared much about pleasing anyone. Ever.

"I'm sorry." I lower my eyes.

"Sorry what?"

"Sorry, sir." I bite my lip as I focus on his shoes, hating more and more as the seconds pass that I upset him in the slightest.

He runs his thumb over my lip. I release it, and he rewards me with a sweet kiss. "Good girl. Go to the turnout room. Wait for me. I'll be there in a few minutes. This meeting won't take long."

I look up at him. "I… thought you wouldn't be on patrol today."

"You think I'm letting my girl be out there alone after the morning you had? Fuck no. I'll take a day of patrol over worrying about you, and how you're handling things being as upset as you are. Now be my good girl and do as you're told."

I smile softly, unsure why obeying him feels so natural to me. Considering just a few weeks ago, the thought of obeying him made bile rise in my throat. Now all I want to do is make him as happy as I can all the time.

"Yes, sir."

He kisses me softly again. "Good girl."

I smile sweetly at him before turning to quickly leave, grabbing my bag on the way. I hurry to the turnout room, but something catches my attention, and I stop to listen.

"Blonde asshole. Looked like he thought he was a prince or some shit. Held himself like he was the Prince of fucking Wales." I hide behind one of the cubicle walls hoping I look casual and not like I'm eavesdropping as one of the officers from night shift talks.

"Cocky as hell. He's like five feet eight. Thinks he's seven feet," another cop says.

"And he took off?" I glance around the corner and see they're talking to a Sergeant. "How the fuck he get away?"

"Realized we suspected him. Took off like a bat out of hell. Had the strangest accent, too. British. But there was something about it. Something different. Fuck. I don't know. We got him on our body cams."

"Download it. Get me an image."

"Yes, Sarge."

I see Mariah coming down the hall looking at me quizzically. "You good?" she asks when she reaches me.

I fall into step with her. "Yeah. I just…" I shake my head. "Just something weird about the description of some guy the night crew is after. Struck me as strange."

"What was so weird?"

"Just… something about it seemed familiar. I don't know." It can't possibly be who I think it is. That's more than improbable. It's impossible. Totally impossible.

"Hmm…" Mariah doesn't look at me, but she doesn't have to. I can feel her senses tingling. Thankfully, she doesn't give me the Mariah Inquisition. "Listen, I was thinking. We haven't been out in awhile. I talked DJ into karaoke tonight. Relieve some stress. You and Matt game?"

I furrow my brows. "How do you do that? Just assume we're together? We haven't told anyone. We've been careful because we wanted to see how it went first."

"You've been together for a couple weeks now, haven't you?"

"Well, yeah, but -"

"No. No 'buts.' You and Matt are perfect together. Karaoke tonight. We're all going."

Knowing Mariah as well as I do, I know arguing is futile. Instead, I follow her to the turnout room and let my mind wander to Matt.

A sexy package.

And he's all for me.

Chapter Six

☆ Matt ☆

I take a long drink of my Michelob Golden Light in my frosted mug and savor the smooth, cold brew making its way down my throat. It's been a long day. Mariah's idea of coming out together for karaoke was a good one. We all need the break. A night of fun to just hang out and be people instead of cops.

I love my job. I'll never not love it. But sometimes the unrelenting public scrutiny for doing my job gets to be a lot. Don't get me wrong. I believe in accountability, but I don't like that there are tens of thousands of cops in this world and the actions of the few are suddenly representative of the actions of all of us. Suddenly a simple traffic stop for a tail light being out becomes a departmental shit storm.

"Matt, don't worry about the complaint. I was there. None of us did anything wrong. Body cams prove it. He's just pissed off because he got tagged for his tint being too dark," Mariah says next to me.

I smile into my glass as I drink down the last of it. "Okay, pint-sized voice of reason," I tease.

She swats me on the arm and laughs. "Jerk."

I put my glass down and turn to her. "How the hell did we become friends? I was a dick to you during your training. Now you're one of the first people I call if I need advice. Or anything for that matter."

"I like to think it's because I'm so awesome, and you just couldn't resist how extraordinary I am." She gives me her best innocent smile before she crosses her eyes and sticks out her tongue.

I laugh. "Okay. Okay. No more dwelling." I look up at DJ. "Come get refills with me. I haven't drank near enough to forget this day."

"Coming from someone who doesn't drink much at all," DJ says as he stands.

"Sometimes a man just needs to lose himself in the cold taste of Michelob." I lean down and kiss Lyric just behind her ear. I've come to learn that it drives her crazy, and the effect it has on her is sexy as hell. I drop my hand to her upper thigh and squeeze, my finger barely grazing her pussy under the table. She lets out a quiet squeak. "And the company of his sexy as hell woman," I whisper in her ear. My breath causes her to shiver. I give her thigh another squeeze as I stand and follow DJ to the bar.

"How's things going with Lyric?" DJ asks when we're out of earshot.

"She's an incredible woman. You both were right. She told me a ton of shit last night. I don't sense that she's holding anything back." I lean my back against the counter and watch Lyric. Seeing her smile and laugh after the night she had lifts my own down in the dump spirits.

DJ hands me mine and Lyrics drinks. "I told you. She's one of a kind."

I watch with pure amusement as DJ and I walk back to the table. There are two men at our table leaning over the backs of mine and DJ's chairs. Mariah and Lyric both have conspiratory looks on their faces. DJ and I hang back within earshot as we watch them.

"They'll never know. Come on. What do they have that I don't, sexy thing?" one of the obviously drunk idiots slurs.

"Hmm...," Lyric begins. "How about a ten inch dick? For starters."

"Size don't mean fuck if you don't know what to do with it," the other idiot says.

"This isn't going to end well," DJ chuckles.

55

I smile and take a drink as I watch and shake my head. "Nope." I know my girl. She may be submissive to me, but no way in hell she'll let these fuckers slide.

"Well, mine has height. You know. Six-four... Big hands. Big feet. You know what they say about a man with big hands and big feet," Mariah says looking over at us. She looks DJ up and down like she wants to lick him.

"Oh! And one more thing," Lyric says, glancing at me. DJ and I move silently until we're right behind both men.

"And what's that?" one of them slur. Lyric says nothing. Just points behind the one standing closest to her. He turns to me, sloshing his beer over the side of his glass, missing Lyric by mere centimeters. "Shit."

"What's up?" I ask towering over him as intimidatingly as possible.

"Need any help finding your way to your table?" DJ growls.

"Nope. No, sir." I don't really know which one says it. Don't really care. Both guys stumble over themselves and make their way to the next table with girls seemingly by themselves.

"What the hell was that about?" I ask as I sit down next to my girl. She leans over and sweetly kisses my shoulder as she sips her Orange Fanta.

"They've been flirting with girls all night. They cornered me and Mariah when we went to the bathroom. They're getting drunker and drunker."

"Bartender keep serving?" DJ asks.

"I haven't seen them go back to the bar," Mariah says, shaking her head. "They've been nursing those beers for a while."

I wince a little at the sound of a dying moose coming from the stage and look up at some drunk blonde trying to sing a Britney Spears tune. She's not the first person who has gone up there thinking she sounds like a pro. I chuckle as she sways her hips and makes eye contact with DJ as she sings.

"Wow. That girl sings like shit," DJ says.

"I think she might be a little in love with you," Mariah teases him as the girl continues to croon directly to DJ.

DJ gives her a cocky smile before tangling his fingers in her hair. "Sucks for her. I'm in love with someone else." He leans down and kisses her as she giggles. The Britney wannabe startles and forgets the words.

"Savage," I say. The girl leaves the stage without finishing the song. I turn to Lyric and lean down.

She leans up and meets my lips. I'm never going to get sick of kissing her. Tasting her sweet tongue when she sneakily pushes it into my mouth to tangle with mine. I suck lightly before pulling away as she softly moans.

"Keep kissing me like that and you'll have me falling in love with you," she says quietly with a shy smile.

"I got news for you, sweet girl. You already are." I kiss her again as her eyes widen. Before she has a chance to say anything, though, the karaoke DJ calls her and Mariah to the stage. I shake my head. "Fuck, I can't believe you two are going to do it."

"Correction. You can't believe I'm going to do it," Lyric says nervously. "Mariah does this all the time."

"I've known her for a while. Never heard her sing." I shake my head. I consider myself pretty brave. I've parachuted out of planes. I run into situations people usually run away from. Singing in front of anyone, especially a bar full of drunk people, is where even I draw the line. She leans down to kiss me again. I give her ass a squeeze. "Good luck."

I watch as Mariah leads Lyric by the hand up to the stage and hands her a microphone. Lyric meets my eyes. I can see the fear, but I know how determined my girl is. I give her an encouraging smile as the music starts and Mariah begins the song.

"Why am I always hit on by the boys I never like? I can always see 'em coming, from the left or from the right," she sings. Her voice is clear, and I can feel my mouth drop as I glance at DJ. He's smiling from ear to ear.

"I don't want to be a priss. I'm just try'na be polite. But it always seems to bite me in the -" Lyric flicks her hips towards the crowd as she turns away to walk around Mariah.

"Ask me for my number, yeah, you put me on the spot," Mariah continues.

"You think that we should hook up, but I think that we should not."

57

"You had me at "hello", then you opened up your mouth." Mariah looks at Lyric and winks.

"And that is when it started going south. Oh!" The two harmonize so well together I have to wonder if maybe Lyric sings with Mariah all the time. *"Get your hands off my hips, 'fore I punch you in the lips. Stop your staring at my... hey! Take a hint, take a hint. No, you can't buy me a drink, let me tell you what I think. I think you could use a mint. Take a hint, take a hint. T-take a hint, take a hint."*

I notice a couple of women that the two guys have flirted with are staring at the stage and starting to sing along. Lyric and Mariah have gained the attention of everyone in the bar. Including the two drunk fucks. I laugh.

"I guess you still don't get it, so let's take it from the top." Mariah meets the eyes of the one who had been drooling all over her only a few minutes ago as she belts out the words. DJ's head bobs to the music as he starts clapping along.

I beam as Lyric does exactly the same thing, gaining confidence as she sings. *"You asked me what my sign is, and I told you it was stop."*

"And if I had a dime for every name that you just dropped."

Lyric nudges Mariah and the two lean against each other. DJ elbows me and points to the back wall. The two drunks look sick. More and more women in the bar are starting to stand and sing. I find myself in complete awe.

Mariah and Lyric start to sing together once more. *"You'd be here and I'd be on a yacht. Oh! Get your hands off my hips, 'fore I punch you in the lips. Stop your staring at my... hey! Take a hint, take a hint. No, you can't buy me a drink, let me tell you what I think. I think you could use a mint. Take a hint, take a hint. T-take a hint, take a hint."*

"What about 'no' don't you get?" Lyric croons. I watch her, unable to get over not only how good she sounds, but how confident she is up there.

"So go and tell your friends."

"I'm not really interested."

"It's about time that you're leavin'."

"I'm gonna count to three and…" Lyric takes Mariah's hand. I lean back in the chair. DJ glances at me. All of the women the guys flirted with are all standing and gathering around the stage.

"It's like a fucking anthem," DJ says to me.

"Leave it to those two to get every woman in the bar to join in their song without them asking."

Both girls are smiling widely as they sing together. "*Open my eyes, and you'll be gone.*"

Lyric holds up one finger and cocks her hip. "*One!*"

"*Get your hands off my ass.*"

Lyric holds up two fingers and cocks her hip to the other side. I can't take my eyes off her. "*Two!*"

"*Or I'll punch you in the dick,*" Mariah improvises.

DJ and I both crack up as the girls send us winks. I glance back at the guys. They both are starting to look more than embarrassed. The red in their face is starting to match the deep red in Lyric's sexy tank top.

Lyric holds up three fingers and cocks her hip again to the other side. My eyes wander hungrily all over her body. "*Three!*"

The women gathered in front of the stage start jumping around like it's a mosh pit singing along with the girls as they sing together to end the song. "*Stop your staring at my... hey! Take a hint, take a hint. I am not your missing link. Let me tell you what I think. I think you could use a mint. Take a hint, take a hint. Take a hint, take a hint. Woah! Get your hands off my hips, 'fore I punch you in the dick! Stop your staring at my... hey! Take a hint, take a hint. T-take a hint, take a hint.*"

The music ends. Lyric and Mariah put the microphones away. I watch as the guys make a hasty exit. Probably a good thing. The women who are all cheering and congratulating the girls probably would have stripped them and paraded them in the street.

"Well, that was hot as fuck," DJ says, adjusting himself as he leans forward to hide what he's doing under the table.

I raise an eyebrow. "That hot, huh?"

He glances down. "Yeah. You should talk."

I laugh and reach down to adjust myself as I watch our girls come back to our table. DJ wastes no time getting up and grabbing Mariah's stuff and her hand.

"DJ?" Mariah asks, slightly confused as he pulls her behind him.

"We're leaving. No arguments. Say goodbye."

I laugh harder as Mariah mumbles a surprised goodbye and nearly runs to keep up with DJ's long stride. Lyric sits next to me and takes a long drink of her Fanta. Her cheeks are flushed a pretty pink. I reach up and tuck a strand of hair behind her ear and lean down to kiss her forehead.

"You did incredible up there."

"I was so scared."

"You almost started a riot. I thought those girls were going to string those guys up in the street and start throwing their burning panties at them."

Lyric laughs as she blushes shyly. "I don't think I was that good. Mariah carried the song. I was terrified. I just followed her."

I shake my head. "Stop selling yourself short. I saw you up there when you hit your groove. Shaking your ass and swinging your hips sassily. You hit every note. Harmonized like a fucking angel. You both were incredible, but you more than held your own, beautiful."

She looks up at me shyly. Submissively. "Thank you."

I choke back a groan and glance to the door. "Ready to head out?"

She nods and takes a last drink of her drink as she slides out of the chair. I take her hand and lead her through the crowd to the exit. We walk through the dark parking lot to my truck. I can't help but notice how she clings to me. It's a little unusual, considering whenever we walk into a call she's as brave as I think I've seen any woman. What it is about her and dark parking lots, though, I'm not really sure.

When we reach my truck, the little resolve I have is completely shattered. She's had me wanting her, all of her, since I woke up with her in my arms this morning. I gently push her against the side of my truck and crush my mouth to hers. She gasps in surprise and moans as she melts into me. I slide my hand down her jeans, shielding her from anyone who may be looking with my body.

I slide two fingers deep inside her sweet, hot pussy at the same time I thrust my tongue into her mouth. She sinks into me with a quiet moan. She grips the waistband of my jeans and the back of my shirt as she spreads her legs for me. I put my leg between hers, deepening the kiss and pressing my dick against her thigh as I thrust my fingers harder and faster into her.

She nips my tongue and moans as her pussy pulses around me. I know she's about to give me what I want, and it takes all of my willpower not to rip her jeans down and bury my face between her legs.

She seems to have the same idea as me. She grips my waistband tighter and grinds against my fingers and leg, making me want to bust through my jeans. I grab her wrist when she tries to unbutton my jeans. I crook my fingers inside her. She whimpers as she trembles, continuing to grind against me. She nibbles on my lip as I pull back.

I kiss up to her ear and whisper, "Come for me. Now."

"Matt!" she scream whispers as she bites my arm. Her pussy clenches as she jerks, soaking my fingers and her panties. I kiss her neck with a low growl. She collapses against the truck, loosening her grip on my shirt as she pants. I slowly thrust her through until she comes down.

"Good girl." I gently remove my fingers from her pussy as I let her go. I help her into the truck as I suck her sweet taste off my fingers.

"How do you make that look so hot?" she asks me wide-eyed.

I smile and lean in to kiss her. "I'm not even close to done with you yet, pretty girl." I nip her lip. She giggles as I pull away and close the door.

I walk over to the driver's side and jump in, taking off and driving us back to my place for the night. She smiles softly the entire drive, and I can't figure out how I managed to get so lucky with her considering all the fuck-ups of my past. Whatever it was I did to deserve her, I'll probably never know.

But I'm fucking glad I did it.

Chapter Seven

☆ Lyric ☆

(Three Days Later)

A few days after our karaoke night, I'm standing under the spray in the shower letting it wash away the night's sleeplessness. The feeling of being dirty. Helpless. Alone.

I shake my head and run my hands over my face before running them through my hair and shutting off the water. I step out to dry off, sniffling a little. I hate having dreams of Hamilton. I hate what he did to me. I hate that he still has the power to instill fear in me.

I look down at my phone when it beeps, signaling a text, and smile at the name that pops on the screen.

Matt.

Matt: Good morning, pretty girl. I'll be over with your latte and Bismarck in ten minutes. I wouldn't mind if you're still in bed.

I laugh and quickly text him back.

Lyric: Sorry. Just took a shower. Getting dressed. Mariah will be here soon. We're going panty shopping.

Matt: You can't hear me, but this is me groaning.

I laugh again, then drop my phone in the sink at the next text that comes through. Matt. Sitting in his truck. His blue jeans unable to hide the sexy, very prominent bulge showing off across his left leg. I cross my legs and rub my thighs together as I bite my lip.

Unfortunately, it doesn't relieve any of the pressure, and I find myself with my hand between my legs playing with my clit as I moan. Before Matt, this was something I'd only done a few times. Since Matt? Ever since I met him, he's been the object of all of the fantasies that play out in my head. Sometimes going to bed, I'll work myself up so much thinking about him that all I need to do is give myself a couple of rubs, and I'm shattering.

I slide two fingers inside myself as I rub my clit with my thumb. I thrust hard and fast, rubbing at the same pace, until I grip the counter so hard I feel like it might break. My pussy quivers as my thighs tremble.

"Fuck!" I lean over the counter just as I'm about to come. There's a hard knock on the door that makes me jump, and I pull away from myself quickly, not wanting Matt to catch me being ridiculous. I've always thought touching myself was such a silly thing to do. But just thinking about Matt... God, he does things to me I can't explain.

I quickly rinse myself off and run out to my bedroom. I grab a pair of bootie shorts and a t-shirt Matt left the last time he stayed with me here. I might need to get him to leave his cologne, though. The shirt doesn't smell like him anymore.

I hurry to my door and peek through the peephole. I furrow my brows when I see no one. Keeping the chain across my door, I slowly open it, peering into the hall. The hair on the back of my neck stands on end. I've learned to trust my instincts, so I very quickly slam the door shut and lock it. I back away from it and run to my room. I'm so on edge because of my dreams, but I know I'm in danger. I can sense it. I can feel it with all of me.

I hear a hard knock again. I choke down a scream as I grab my gun. I won't let him get me this time. I won't. Hamilton may know where I am, but he'll never get to me. I'll never be his victim again.

I jump at another knock and throw a hand over my mouth. My heart beats out of control. He said last night in a text that he's coming for me. My hands are shaking. I'm trembling. I force my grip on my gun to

63

steady as I make my way to the door. I shakily pull the chain off the door and unlock it, preparing to face the man who has thrown my new life into a tailspin.

Taking a deep breath, I throw the door open and back away several steps. I point my gun at the door. All of the blood rushes to my ears like a freight train.

"Whoa! Whoa! Baby, what the fuck are you doing?" Matt raises his hands defensively in front of him, but I know it's to show me that he has nothing in them. "Lyric," he says soothingly, his deep voice cutting through the chaos in my head. "Baby, look at me. Listen to my voice." He looks me directly in my eyes, forcing me to steady the tiny little fighter jets racing through my veins. He keeps his hands out in front of him and doesn't move from the door. "It's me. You know I'm not going to hurt you. Can you see me, honey? Look at me."

I slowly nod, letting myself come back down to Earth. I gradually lower my gun, my hands quaking. I start sobbing and drop to my knees. The gun clatters to the floor as I cover my face with my hands. Matt's arms are around me in an instant. He pulls me against his chest and tugs me up.

"I'm so sorry!" My fingers grip his shirt so hard I feel like I could rip it in half, but I don't care. I feel like I'm about to fall off the edge of a cliff into a deep abyss.

"Shh… I got you, baby. I'm right here. But we need to leave. Now."

"W-what?"

"I'll explain outside. We need to get out of here. Right now."

I have no idea what's going on, but I trust him. I let him lead me outside through the throngs of people in the hallway. Cops. Firefighters. Men in military uniforms. Face after face of confused souls.

Matt keeps me tucked into his side as I tremble. Everything around me seems to go in slow motion. The voices. Us walking. The activity around us.

I close my eyes and stumble my way along as Matt rushes me away from the apartment building. I let him because I can't think. It isn't until we're across the street that I can't physically hold myself up anymore. Even with Matt's help. I collapse into a sobbing mess on the grass.

Matt drops with me, tugging me to his chest. He kisses my neck and tangles one of his hands in my hair. The other digs into my hip. I

64

shudder and shiver against him seemingly for hours while he hugs me and whispers soothingly in my ear. I bury myself in Matt's chest, making myself as small as I possibly can as I curl into him as closely as my body will let me.

"Hey. It's okay. Honey, look at me." He tugs my hair so I look up at him, though I'm trembling uncontrollably. "I'm here. No one is getting through me. No one. Do you trust me?"

I nod and sniffle as I take a deep breath. "I trust you."

"Then trust me when I tell you that you're safe."

I jump and whimper at the chaotic scene. People yelling. Sirens wailing. "Matt…"

"Matt! Lyric! Fuck, are you guys okay?" DJ asks, dropping down next to us.

I nod gripping Matt for dear life, though I don't really know if I'm okay or not. I don't understand what's happening. I still haven't completely come back to myself, so I do what I've learned to do over the years. I force myself to think logically. Step by step. It's the only way to keep myself from falling apart.

I know Hamilton knows where I am. I've gotten clues and signs over the past couple of months. Things I've never mentioned to anyone. Things I needed to figure out for myself. The phone calls. Dreams. They're just the tip of the iceberg.

Mariah launches herself at me. "Holy shit, Lyric! Are you okay?" She looks me up and down, lifting the back of my shirt and studying me like a science experiment. "What's happening? What happened?"

DJ grabs Mariah around the waist and pulls her to him still kneeling next to us. Matt sits, tugging me into his lap. DJ follows suit, pulling Mariah into his as he sits on the grass next to Matt.

"Brody is directing that whole scene over there. What the fuck happened?" DJ asks.

Matt hugs me a little tighter. "I got here a little while ago with coffee and the rolls she likes. There was a box by her door so I bent to pick it up. I got a whiff of gunpowder. Dropped the coffee as I knocked on the door. I called you and texted Payton to get his dog over here."

"G-gunpowder?" My head feels like it might explode. It's pounding with more thoughts and scenarios than I can keep up with.

Gunpowder? What is he trying to do? Blow me up? Matt's grip tightens as he cuddles me into his chest.

"What? What the fuck is going on? What am I missing?" DJ asks. I can feel him tense even though he's not touching me.

"Lyric, what is going on? I know there's something you haven't told me," Mariah says tearfully.

I hide in Matt's chest. Because she's right, and I'm ashamed. I should have told her. I shouldn't have kept it from her or DJ. I shouldn't have kept it from Matt. I shouldn't have been stupid enough to think I could do this all on my own. Why? Why do I always think I can do this all by myself?

"Lyric? Lyric!" I look up at Brody barreling towards me like the impenetrable force of nature that he is. He drops to his knees and pulls me away from Matt slamming me against his chest as he hugs me.

Hard.

Tight.

"What the hell do you think you're doing?" Matt growls.

"Hugging my fucking daughter. You got an issue with it, you can try and stop me. Guarantee you won't win," Brody growls right back.

"Daughter? You're her…? What the fuck is going on?" Matt asks, bewildered.

"Have you… not told him?" Brody asks me. I shake my head. So much. I've kept so much from him. All of them. It makes me sick. "Everyone up. We're leaving."

"No! No. I want to know what the fuck is happening!" Matt bellows.

"Not here, Chance." Brody stands and helps me up. He tucks me close to his side.

I'm too tired to fight and too scared to look up at Matt or Mariah or DJ. I don't need to look at them to see how much I have hurt them by not being honest with them. I can almost feel the damage I've done pouring off of them. It's not that I don't trust them enough to tell them. They, and Brody, are the very few that I trust implicitly. Truth is, I'm scared. Scared that if I tell them… they'll get drawn into his games. That they will get hurt. First Tyler, then Brody both tore down the barriers I tried to build around myself. Then Mariah, DJ and now Matt have begun to do the same. And I'm terrified that they will get hurt because of me.

After a short drive away from the apartment building, we all climb out of Brody's car and make our way into his house. He locks all of the doors and draws all of the shades before he turns to all of us. I sit in a chair, curling myself up as tightly as I can. Matt stands by the door. DJ and Mariah huddle together on the couch. Brody stands by the window and heaves a long sigh.

"What is going on? Everything. I'm not asking again." Matt doesn't make a move towards me. He sounds angrier and angrier. It radiates off him and slams into me.

"Sit down, Matt," Brody says tiredly.

"I'll stand. Thanks."

"Matt! Sit down," Brody commands. "Do you not see what you're doing to her?"

I close my eyes when Matt looks at me. "Fuck. Baby." He rushes to me and tugs me out of the chair. He sits and pulls me into his lap. I burrow into him, tucking myself in his arms as closely as I can.

"I'm so sorry," I whisper into his shoulder as I lock my arms around him.

"Shh… Don't. Don't talk. Brody. Please. Just tell me what the hell is going on. I'm made of questions." Matt runs his fingers through my hair and hugs me close to him. I deflate with relief.

"A couple of years ago, I got a phone call from a cop in the United Kingdom. His name is Tyler. About ten years ago, Tyler and I ended up working a case. Car theft ring. Tracked it to the United Kingdom. Tyler was my contact before Interpol took my case. We stayed in touch, became friends, though neither of us knew what happened with the car theft ring. Interpol kept it under lock and key. Our security clearance with international cases doesn't go that high."

"Brody, I appreciate that you have friends in other countries, but what the hell does that have to do with any of this?" Matt asks.

"I'm getting to that. You want the whole story? Shut up and listen."

"Just… talk, Brody. Please. We all want to know what's happening with her. Obviously she's far too scared of something to tell us," Mariah says quietly.

"You're right. There's a lot of shit that happened in the United Kingdom. I don't know how much you know, so I'll start at the

67

beginning." Brody takes a deep breath. I inhale Matt's cologne and close my eyes. "Lyric was training to be a cop in the UK. Before her training ended, she became a victim of stalking. Another officer took an interest in her. They went out once. She didn't make a connection. He didn't like that. It got to the point where he'd become physical with her at work. He was fired. She wasn't the only woman he'd become obsessed with. But she was the only one he'd taken it one step further with. She drove home one night. Saw her house had been set on fire."

"We knew that," DJ says.

Brody nods. I'm starting to shiver. Matt hugs me tighter. I can sense Brody sitting on the couch across from us. "Tyler was her training officer. They'd become close. He let her stay with him. Her family life was… well, fucked up. There's no other way to describe it. She had no one. Just him. Lyric was upset. Obviously. She'd lost everything. She had to take time off. Put her training on hold. She basically locked herself away. Hid. When she was ready to come out of hiding, he came back for her. Tyler was at work. He broke into the house. Beat the hell out of Lyric."

My body convulses as I start sobbing. The tears I fought so hard to keep at bay burst like a dam. I grip Matt's collar. He tangles his fingers in my hair. I feel more arms encircling me, but I can't bear the thought of opening my eyes. I don't want to see the pity; the disappointment in me for keeping so much hidden. Brody is getting to the part that only he and Tyler know. I don't know how Matt, DJ, or Mariah are going to take it, but I'm terrified they'll all leave. That Hamilton will win once more in taking away my entire world.

"Hamilton, Lyric's nightmare, ran. Police couldn't find him. His family is well to do. They helped hide him. Nothing we can prove, but we know. Lyric had always wanted to visit the United States. Tyler decided that she wasn't safe in the United Kingdom. He moved with her to a safehouse while they got her a Visa and started her citizenship paperwork. The battle with immigration began. Tyler knew they couldn't wait for her citizenship to be approved. So he contacted me. We worked together and got her here. She did a lot of traveling before we finally got her citizenship approved. They fought with us on calling her a refugee. They fought us on every step we took. But we finally got it dealt with. We got Lyric

68

permanent residence here. When she came back here between the travels she did here, she stayed with me."

"This is why you got so defensive when I had an issue training her." I can feel Matt shake his head as he rubs his hands up and down my back. "I'm sorry, baby. I wish you would've told me this."

"He's not done," I whisper against his throat. "Please, please don't hate me."

"Jesus. Lyric. I won't hate you. I could never hate you. I'm too fucking in love with you to ever hate you."

It becomes so quiet, a pin could drop and sound like a bomb. My heart physically hurts because I don't think he'll love me anymore when Brody tells him all I've hidden. But he needs to know how I feel about him. Even if he throws me away.

"I love you, too, Matt. You don't know how much."

I sniffle as Brody begins speaking once more. "Lyric flourished. She'd started to come out of her shell. Started to become her old self. A spitfire. Hell on wheels. Tyler was happy to see it. I was ecstatic to know she was starting to feel safe and secure. Trust that Tyler and I weren't giving up on finding Hamilton. But a few months ago, she started getting phone calls. At first just breathing. Then a couple words to scare her. Shit like he knew where she lived. He's coming for her. She started having dreams again. Reliving all that happened. And then a couple of weeks ago... she got a package delivered to headquarters."

"What?" Matt pushes me back just enough to look at me. I cling harder to him, white-knuckling his shirt as I bite my lip and whimper like a wounded wolf pup. Just when I think he's going to shove me off his lap, he pulls me back to his chest so hard that, for a moment, I think he may crack my ribs. "Fucking hell."

"I called her into my office. I had intervened. The package was given to me since I'm her Captain. But I had it checked. I opened it. It was a ring. Turns out, it was her grandmother's ring. A ring that she thought was lost in the fire. A claddagh ring. It was one of the only things she had left of her grandmother. Her grandmother had been the only person in her family to ever give a shit about her, so that ring meant a lot to her. The ring was cut in half. Laying in a small box in two pieces."

"Lyric...," Matt whispers in my ear. "Why didn't you tell me?"

"I was scared..."

69

"Of what? Baby, I could've helped you."

"I didn't want you to get hurt. I didn't want anyone to get hurt." I say the words so only he can hear me. He tangles my hair around his hand and rocks me in his arms.

"Jesus Christ," he whispers in my hair. I can feel him shaking against me, so I hug him just as tightly as he is me as he kisses my forehead.

"That's not all, Matt," Brody says quietly.

"What else could there possibly be? Fuck," DJ breathes. I can hear the sadness, the heartbreak in his voice. Mariah and DJ are still locked around me just as Matt is. I sink into their embrace, starting to relax with the knowledge of knowing that they aren't going to run, but still tense with the idea they might get hurt if they get too close to me and my fucked up world.

"Hamilton. We thought we tracked him. We thought he was in Paris. He's not. He's... Fuck... He's here. We tracked him here. We don't know where. We just know he's in the United States. Somewhere."

"He's here... He has to be," I whisper.

"We've been trying to find him, but he's good at hiding," Brody continues. "When you got the first package we thought we found him. But he slipped away. Since it was sent to the department and postmarked from the UK, we were thrown."

"This one wasn't postmarked. It was a plain box," Matt says.

"Which means we need a plan. He's here. Has to be. We know he's probably watching her," Brody says. The couch cushions crinkle as he leans forward on the couch. DJ pulls away but stays close. Mariah shifts and lays her head on my stomach, keeping her arms locked around my waist. Matt's arms encompass the rest of me.

"She can stay with me," DJ says.

"Fuck that. She's staying at my house," Matt growls.

"Matt, think about that. DJ is right. He knows where Lyric lives. He's following her. No way he doesn't know where you live." Brody stands and locks his hands behind his head as he walks around his living room thinking.

"Of all of us, my house is a fortress," DJ says. "Behind Matt. His house is Fort Knox."

"All the more reason for her to be there," Matt argues.

"Do I get a say?" I ask meekly.

"No!" all the guys say in unison.

"The hell she doesn't," Mariah says as she reluctantly lets me go and stands. "It's Lyric's life that this guy is fucking with. She should get a choice in where she stays. She's the one who needs to feel safe."

Matt takes a deep breath to calm himself. "She's right. I'm sorry, baby."

"I want to stay with you. I don't want to be away from you." I shift slightly and look up at him. He leans in and kisses me with a soft smile. He smooths my hair down and wipes my eyes with the pad of his thumb when he pulls away. "I don't feel safe at my apartment. And for once I don't want to argue and do it all on my own."

"You don't have to. You're never going to have to do anything on your own again, Lyric." Matt leans forward and kisses me again, and I melt into him, finally completely relaxed.

I've never trusted anyone implicitly other than Tyler and Brody and my nana. But over the few months that I've known the small group of people surrounding me, I've come to trust each of them more and more. They've each managed to remove a brick of my wall until it's collapsed.

Now that it has, I don't want to let any of them go. All I want is to surround myself with them and let them in. It surprises me to know that I'm not afraid of my wall collapsing for them. What does surprise me is the ease with which they've all replaced the wall I've built to protect myself with their own impenetrable wall. One they've built with their own bodies.

And I've never felt safer.

Chapter Eight

★ Matt ★

(One Week Later)

"Entry team, on my count," I say to my team. "Three. Two. Enter!"

DJ kicks in the door, and we all follow him inside, staying low to the ground. Shots ring out around us, but we push forward.

"I'm not coming out of here alive!" someone screams. More bullets bury in the walls around us. We stay low and close to the opposite wall. "You won't take me alive!"

"Fuck, I'm done with this guy," DJ says into our earpieces.

"Maintain positions," I command. "Follow the plan."

DJ peeks around the corner and more shots ring out. "Fuck me." He lays prone on the ground with his AR-15 pointed into the room.

"You're our eyes, DJ. What do you see?"

"He's walking around mumbling to himself. Tugging his hair," DJ nearly whispers. "He's dropped the gun. I don't see any other visible weapons. Now's our chance."

"Surround. Take him down. No shots unless he fires. Go!" I command.

We all move like one cohesive unit. Our weapons are drawn. There is a flurry of movement and activity. Everyone is screaming at once for him to get on the ground. I'm laser focused on him. His hands are on his head. He's still pulling his hair. Screaming. Two of my guys bring him quickly to the ground and cuff him while I secure the gun he dropped. He's led out to a waiting squad car.

DJ stands next to me. "Of all the SWAT calls I've been on, I don't think I've seen anything like that in my life."

I take a deep breath and take my helmet off. "Why the fuck do calls like this have to happen on days when I actually want to be on the fucking streets?"

DJ takes his helmet off and rests his hand on my shoulder. "She's with Mariah. She'll be okay."

"It isn't that I think she'll get hurt. It's that he knows where she is. He's been following her for days. Weeks. Maybe even months. I don't like that she's out there at all."

"You mean you don't like that she's out there without you."

I look over at him before letting out a long sigh. "Yeah. Without me. I'm in love with that girl. Fuck if I know when it happened, but I'm not complaining. She's…" I look back across the living room as we start walking out of the house. "She's everything to me, DJ. I don't know what I'd do if anything happened to her."

"You'd probably destroy the universe. I know because I feel the same with Mariah. But you also need to trust that she knows what she's doing and is capable of getting help if she needs it. You think I'm not concerned that Mariah is being put in just as much danger? I am. But I have to trust that she and Lyric will rely on each other and their training if they have to."

"Think she'd be pissed if I called her back into the office and made her sit behind a desk until this Hamilton asshole is caught?"

"Well, think about that a second." We both jump into the squad with our mentally unwell suspect. DJ starts driving towards the hospital with the guy screaming in the backseat. "Do you think Mariah would let me pull her if this were her?"

"Fuck no. She'd throw a fit."

"So would Lyric. You can't keep her from doing what she loves. We have no real reason to pull her. He hasn't threatened her while she's been working. If she starts getting those phone calls when she's on shift, and he starts saying he knows where she is when she's taking calls, then Brody won't hesitate to pull her."

"The problem is she hasn't been too forthcoming up to this point." The guy in the back starts banging his head on the plexiglass between the back and front seat. Fed up with him and dealing with his antics the past three hours, I turn and slap the glass. "Enough!" The plexiglass vibrates against his head, and he looks at me with wide eyes. "One more outburst, and I tell the psych ward to commit you for the rest of your fucking life. Capish?"

He sits back and looks at me. "Yes, sir."

"Fuck," I growl under my breath.

"The reason she hasn't been so forthcoming," DJ continues, "is because she's been trying to keep us all away from it. She didn't want us involved. Didn't want us getting hurt. You can't tell me that you and I wouldn't do the same thing. And you know Mariah would."

"I know. I know. Doesn't make this shit easier."

"My advice? When we get back to headquarters, call her in. Go out there with her."

"We'll have an extra squad on the streets. Brody won't let that fly."

"Seems to me he'd make an exception when it comes to her." DJ pulls into the Emergency Bay, and we both get out of the car. A doctor and nurse meet us with a bed while DJ and I pull the guy out of the squad car.

"Injuries?" the doctor asks.

"Hit his head against the plexiglass on the way over here. Other than that no," I say.

The doctor checks out his head, using a pen light to check his eyes for any signs of a concussion. "How many times?"

"Three. I smacked the glass the last time and scared him. He sat back like a good boy the rest of the drive."

The doctor chuckles. "Get his cuffs off so we can strap him down. You can cuff him to the bar when he's situated. You have an officer staying?"

74

"We have someone on the way," DJ says. "Should be here any minute. I'll relay where he is."

"I'll have him in ER room eleven. Need to check him before we take him up."

"You want us to stay, or is hospital security good with him?" I ask.

"Security is on the way here. We can wait to uncuff him if you want. Saves us from having to switch out cuffs."

"I'd appreciate it," I say.

Moments later, hospital security strolls out to the bay, and I force down the growl making its way up my throat. Like we don't have anything better to do with our day then wait for them. They knew we were coming. The fucking doctor and a nurse, who are both probably really busy, can be here waiting for us. But security can't? No wonder when shit goes down in the hospital, they call Gainesville PD first. We usually get there before their security does, though they're in the same building.

"Thank you officers. We can take it from here," one of the security officers says. He takes the cuffs belonging to one of my officers off. DJ and I look at him incredulously.

Security takes their sweet ass time cuffing him to the bed. DJ and I stand back with our arms folded over our chest. Waiting. We've been dealing with this guy for over three hours now. He's prone to outbursts, and he's about due.

Just as we thought, he starts flailing. He flings himself off the bed, tipping it over since only one of his hands are secured. The doctor and nurse both jump back further than they already were. DJ and I look at each other and casually pull the doctor and nurse towards us, enjoying the show.

The guys screams and swings at security, fighting with them until they are finally able to get him cuffed to the bed. They finish strapping him down as he yells obscenities and makes demonic growling noises. Both security officers look up at us.

"Could've helped, don't you think? Or are you too busy digesting those breakfast donuts?" the smart ass glares at me.

I growl dangerously and narrow my eyes as I take a step towards them. DJ holds me back and pushes me towards the squad. "Not worth it, Chance. Let's go."

"Maybe if you fuckers weren't so fucking lazy, we wouldn't have to call PD here all the damn time," the doctor says for me. Both security officers blush in embarrassment as I crack up. The doctor winks at me as they all push the screaming man into the building. "Room eleven!" the doctor calls back over his shoulder as the doors close.

I duck into the squad and grab the radio, barking orders for the officer we have coming here to stand guard during the guys exam.

"Fuck, I swear you cause chaos wherever you go. People just naturally don't like you," DJ teases.

"Maybe if people didn't inherently suck, I wouldn't have to be a dick. And I don't think they liked you either, asshole."

"Everyone likes me." He gives me a cocky grin and a wink. I laugh, thinking for the millionth time that I'm glad we ended up becoming friends. DJ is one of the few people who can keep my temper from exploding into a fiery fulmination.

I shake my head. "Get me back to HQ."

"Yes, sir, Lieutenant, sir."

I laugh again as I pick up the radio. "SWAT One to Squad Thirty-two.."

"Go ahead," Mariah's perky voice comes over the radio.

"Head back to HQ. We'll meet you there."

"Yes, Lieutenant."

"You feel better now?" DJ asks.

"I'll feel better once I have my girl in my arms. It was bad enough I couldn't convince her to disappear with me for a few days."

"Lyric isn't one to run. She's done that her whole life. I think she's at the point now where she'll get scared for a little while, but she'll fight. She doesn't have any flight left in her."

I smile because I know he's right. My girl is tough. It's one of the things that I've always found so attractive about her. I know she can handle herself. Still doesn't solve my insatiable need to be that barrier between her and whatever danger comes her way. She's fought alone for too long. I'm never letting her fight alone again.

76

"Matt. Take a look at this," Brody says, dropping down in a chair in front of my desk. He slides a folder across it to me. I hesitantly open it already knowing I'm not going to like what I'm about to see.

"You going to give me a hint on what's in here?"

"No. I know how much you like surprises."

"Fuck. I hate surprises."

"That's not entirely true. Lyric certainly seems to be a surprise you enjoy."

I smile despite myself. "Where is my girl anyway?"

"They got pulled to a call on the way in. It was priority. She's on the way in now."

I nod as I open the folder. I flip through, growing more and more confused. "What the fuck am I looking at? Looks like a bunch of stolen luxury cars."

"All from the UK. All between three and five years ago."

I look up at him suspiciously. "Where are you going with this?"

He nods to the folder. "Keep going. Tell me what you see."

I look down and flip through the rest of the pages, shifting uncomfortably. I lean forward resting my elbows on the desk. "It looks like we have some luxury cars being stolen all throughout the US and the UK."

"Yep. That's the big picture."

I read through some of the reports and look at the sketch of the suspect and the image from our officer's body cams. "Sketch matches what we got pretty well. You thinking this is related?"

"Not thinking. I know." He leans forward and puts the images together. "I know sketches ain't always accurate, but sure looks similar to me. This sketch is what I got from Tyler. This image is from our body cams. And this..." He flips to the end of my file. "This is Hamilton Prescott."

My heart skips a beat. "Are you fucking kidding me?"

Brody shakes his head and leans back in the chair with his arms crossed over his chest. "Not kidding. This is a huge fucking breakthrough."

I dive into the file with new interest. "So the UK thinks Prescott is involved with this luxury car ring."

"Not just involved. They think he's running it."

I smirk and chuckle. "Pretty little rich boy don't have enough trust fund money?"

"Very funny. Now look and tell me what you see."

"Well, he's moved it over here. Obviously. Looks to be a huge ring. Nationwide." I flip back through a few more pages and read some reports. "Miami PD thought they had him. He escaped. We have evidence of him being here. What more do you want me to see?"

"Matt. Come on. You didn't make Lieutenant because Chief thinks you're pretty. You made Lieutenant because you're smart."

I sigh and rub my temples. And then I see it. "Holy shit."

"Yep."

I look up at him. "Are you fucking serious?"

"Mmhmm."

"We need to get on this." I stand and start grabbing my gear, but Brody stands and puts his hand on my arm to stop me.

"Matt. No. We're on this. Your job is to keep this from Lyric. She doesn't get involved. That's final. She stays far away from this. I have officers already in motion."

"Who?"

"DJ is one of them. I knew that would put your mind at ease." He lets go of my arm, and I let out a breath. "We're going to get him."

"This deal you think he has going down right now better be this guy's end. Because if Prescott gets to Lyric, I'll take everyone down with me."

"You can't think you're the only one."

I look up as Lyric appears in my doorway. "Hey, baby." I force a smile.

She raises an eyebrow and looks at me with so much suspicion that I actually feel guilty. "Who isn't the only one?"

I choke down the deep breath I want to take. More to steady myself. "It's just a case I've been working on."

"A case? What case?"

"Theft. We think we caught the guy. Case has been bugging us for awhile now," Brody jumps in. I mentally thank him.

Lyric, however, doesn't look convinced, but, thankfully, she doesn't push it. "Okay. Well, I'm here. What did you need to see me for?"

"Actually, I did, honey," Brody says, saving my ass again. "We're sending you home for the day."

"Why?"

"It came from higher powers. With everything that happened with you being threatened, the department has decided that you need to be off for a while."

"What?" she sputters. "That's completely ridiculous! It hasn't been affecting my job! We already agreed that I would have my partner with me in my squad!"

I shoot Brody a glare. I knew that wouldn't fly. "Baby, it's for the day. That's it. The department needs to change things around to allow for me to ride with you. That means cases I have pending need to get assigned to someone else because I can't work them."

"I don't need a bodyguard! I was fine out there with Mariah!" she very nearly screams at me. I look over her head and see the crowd forming watching us.

I tug her into the office and slam the door, glaring at the onlookers. "Lyric, stop it. I know you're capable of taking care of yourself. So does Brody."

"Then why are you treating me like a little kid who needs to be protected?" She crosses her arms and narrows her eyes at me.

I lower my voice and stand over her, looking down at her just as fiercely as she is me. "I'm treating you no differently than I would Mariah if it were her in this situation," I say in my most dominant tone. She immediately softens as I continue, not changing my stance or my tone. "Would you want me to send her out by herself or with you knowing that DJ is back here worrying himself sick about her?"

"No, sir," she whispers submissively as she looks at me through her lashes.

I reach up and tuck a strand of loose hair behind her ear. She nuzzles into my palm and closes her eyes. "I'm not doing this because I don't trust that you can handle yourself. I'm doing this because I'm worried as fuck about you. And so is the department. We all want to make sure you're safe. We'd do this for anyone. But I have a vested interest." I tug at her vest. "You're carrying what's mine underneath here."

She blushes. "I'm sorry. I just -"

"I know, honey. You don't like being controlled." I lean down to whisper in her ear. "At least if we're not in the bedroom." She shifts and rubs her legs together as I pull away.

79

"Lyric, just trust us," Brody says from behind me. I had nearly forgotten he was in the room. "We're doing what's best for you. Go home for the day. I hate the idea of you coming back at all until this is over, but it's obvious I'm not going to get my way on that."

Lyric shakes her head, like she's coming out of a submissive daze. She blinks a few times before turning to Brody. "I won't let him control my life like that anymore. I quit a job I loved because of him. He took my whole life from me. I'll never let him do that to me again."

Brody nods and gives her a quick hug before he gives me a look that says to keep my mouth shut. He heads for the door and quietly closes it behind him. I pull Lyric close because I need to feel her. I've been away from her for too long. She may not like the idea of a bodyguard, but I won't let her out there without me. If she insists on continuing with her life as normally as she can, I'll admire her for it. Hell, I'll support it.

But no way in hell will she be doing it if I'm not right next to her.

Chapter Nine

☆ Lyric ☆

(One Week Later)

I mix melted cheese and salsa in the crockpot I have sitting on the counter and peek at the TV from the kitchen as Matt and DJ both start yelling.

"Fuck! Come on! What the hell kind of a call was that?" Matt yells as he throws peanut M&M's at the screen.

"You're fucking blind, ref!" DJ yells as he stands. He turns and heads for the kitchen as I shake my head and smile softly. He grabs a beer from the fridge before heading back to the couch and tossing one to Matt.

I put the lid back on the crockpot and grab a soda from the fridge. I grab one for Mariah and head outside to the pool where she's tanning on one of the loungers. I can't help but laugh as I sit down next to her and hand her the drink. She takes it gratefully and looks at me quizzically.

"Here I am parading around in sexy booty shorts and a Tampa Bay Buccaneers jersey trying to distract my boyfriend long enough to get him to ease the pressure between my legs. And here you are in your bra and panties tanning on the deck in DJ's line of sight. Maybe I'm doing it all wrong."

Mariah laughs and takes a long drink of her soda. "You won't get either of them away from the screen until the game is done. Football is like their lifeblood. They feed off it. You should see them during the off season."

I tilt my head curiously. "What are they like during off season?"

"They mope around like they have nothing to live for and watch any sport that comes on TV just to pass the time."

I laugh. "God, I hope you're joking."

"Maybe a little. But seriously. Football is life."

I settle back into the pool chair and sip my soda, focusing on the pool. "So? How are things with DJ?"

"Amazing. DJ is remarkable. He gets me. He just… fits. You know? I never thought I'd ever find that."

I smile softly. "I'm glad. You guys really do make an amazing couple."

She looks up at me. "What about you? How's things going with Matt? And I mean really going. I don't want the 'things are fine' answer."

"Matt is… he's one of a kind. I guess I never really knew what I was missing until him. I sort of thought I'd never find someone. But I realized that I was just waiting around for him. It's like some weird fairytale I never thought I'd ever live. I still can't really believe it."

"To be honest… As soon as I met you, I knew you and Matt belonged together."

I look at her and furrow my brows. "How could you have known that? I hated him when I first met him."

She shakes her head. "No… You really didn't. And as much as you and he want to believe it, neither did he. Matt has always been attracted to you. Just like you were to him."

She closes her eyes and looks up towards the sun. I can't figure out how she's so instinctual. It's completely crazy to me that she just… knows things. That she can sense them so quickly and figure things out as fast as she does.

"I don't understand how you do that. How you just know things."

"I know people. I don't like people, oddly enough, considering my profession. But I know people. I can read them. And I know you and Matt.

82

You're both incredible people who deserve happiness and all the love the world has to offer."

I smile and look up as Matt appears in the doorway. His arms are folded across his chest, and he's watching me with a soft smile on his face as he leans against the frame. I blush when I see the heat in his eyes. I watch as he looks me up and down then gestures me to him with a finger. Mariah giggles as DJ slides past Matt and makes his way out to the pool deck. His eyes are focused completely on her.

I gravitate towards Matt like his magnetic field is pulling me to him. I feel like I'm floating across the deck. When his hand reaches for mine, and he turns and leads me into the house, my mind can focus on nothing but him.

He leads me into a hallway and stops, pushing me back against the wall. I look up at him submissively. "Did you think you in this Buccs jersey and those sexy as fuck tight shorts did nothing for me?" His hands trail up my thighs to my hips. His thumbs tuck in the waistband of the shorts. He looks at me hungrily.

I run my hands up his muscular arms to his massive shoulders and bite my lip. I swallow hard, trying to moisten my suddenly dry throat. "I was hoping it would."

He leans in to kiss me as he tugs the shorts down inch by torturously slow inch. He kisses down my jaw to my neck and nips the tender skin. I moan and melt into him, digging my fingers into his shoulders. His tongue swipes across my collarbone as he kisses it, moving his way down. My shorts slide down more and more as he sinks to his knees in front of me. He looks up at me as he removes them completely. I start to remove the jersey, but he stops me with a single, dark look.

"Did I say to do that?"

I lick my lips. "No…"

"Good girl. Spread your legs for me." My body follows his command like it has no choice. And it doesn't. He's in control now. Just the way I need him to be. Just as I crave him to be. I'm already quivering for him, and he hasn't even touched me.

He leans forward and licks his way up my thigh, leaving kisses along the way. Just as he gets to the point where I want him the most, he stops. He moves to the other thigh and does the same thing until he gets to my waiting center. He looks up at me.

I whimper. "Matt, please," I say in less than a whisper. I can barely hear myself.

He smiles and slowly licks from my pussy to my clit as he hums. "Mmm... Don't you taste sweet?"

"Oh, God." My fingers tangle in his hair, and I tug. He licks slowly from my pussy to my clit again and again until I'm writhing, silently begging him to give me more. His fingers. His tongue. Him. All of him. Just when I think I can't take anymore, he thrusts his tongue hard into me. I scream, "Matt!"

"Mmm... Baby, you're soaked."

"Dripping. For you. Only for you."

He swirls his tongue inside me. I grip his hair and pull him closer against me as I grind against his tongue. My pussy clenches hard around him and pulses with every swipe of his magical tongue. My thighs shake.

"Not yet." He pulls back and grips the backs of my thighs as he stands.

I nearly cry at being denied the release I desperately need. "Matt! Please!"

"Shh. Be a good girl, and you'll get what you want. Don't follow my commands, and I'll come inside you and refuse to let you."

His mouth crashes against mine, effectively cutting off any and all arguments I had thought to utter. He lifts me off the ground and holds me between his body and the wall, never taking his lips off mine. I wrap my legs tightly around his waist. My arms lock around his shoulders.

Still kissing me, his tongue dominating mine, Matt reaches between us to unbutton his cargo shorts. My entire body erupts into an inferno of need. He teases my pussy with his tip, rubbing it against my clit. I whimper and moan, scratching at his shoulders as my pussy trembles for him. He pulls back from the kiss, leaving me dazed, and watches me.

"Tell me what you want." He moves his tip slowly against me.

I throw my head back in frustration. "You! Matt, please. You! I want you!"

"Look at me, pretty girl."

I look at him, my body becoming weaker as I shake and shiver. All of his touches and intense looks drive me to near madness.

Just when I think I'm going to die, Matt slides his glorious dick deep inside me. "Ah! Matt! Oh, fuck yes!" I writhe against him, my body

84

fighting to ride him until we both collapse. My mind, though, knows he needs to dominate. I try to be good, but it's hard when he feels the way he does. When I crave him as much as I do.

Matt gives me no time to adjust to his ten inch and perfectly thick cock buried balls deep inside me. He immediately starts plunging hard, slamming my back against the wall with every deep thrust. He pulls himself all the way out, making me yearn for him even more, then crashes himself back into me again. And again. And again.

I pant against his neck, holding onto him as he takes me on the ride of my life. His fingers dig into my ass as he buries his face in my hair. He lifts me every time he pulls out, and slams me down again every time he drives back into me. I lose all the control I never had to begin with as he directs and monopolizes all of my movements. I submit to him completely, my pussy clenching and pulsing with every ram of his dick.

"Come for me. Do it now."

"Oh, God! Matt! Ah!" I scream his name and follow his command. I come so hard that my hips jerk against his. My pussy bucks over his dick as he sinks himself deep inside me. He comes so hard, I'm nearly lifted off him with the force.

"Fuck! Lyric!" Matt leans into me and against the wall. He gently bites into my shoulder as he slows his thrusts. He growls low. My pussy pulses and clenches again.

"Matt…," I whimper as I come a second time. His hips continue to jerk gently against mine as we both come down panting against each other's necks.

After several moments, Matt pulls slowly out of me. He gently sets me on my feet and kneels to grab my shorts. He helps me back into them, giving my pussy a long lick, and my clit a kiss before he stands and pulls my shorts all the way up. He leans in to kiss me. I moan almost silently at the tangy taste of myself on his tongue.

He pulls back slowly and takes a step back, leaving one hand on my waist. I look at him curiously as he peeks around the corner and chuckles. He looks back at me and kisses my cheek. "Go get cleaned up and changed baby. You have time."

I tilt my head slightly. "Time?"

"Yes. Time. DJ is still fucking Mariah on the pool deck."

My mouth drops, and I blush as I hurry to the bathroom. Behind me, Matt laughs as he tucks himself away. I close the door behind me and lean against it, closing my eyes and taking several deep breaths. I find myself smiling as I come down from my sex-induced daze.

I hurry to clean up and find a pair of shorts in the linen closet in the bathroom. Matt always keeps extra shorts and sweats in all of the bathrooms in his house. It's come in handy considering how many times we find ourselves unable to keep our hands off each other and our bodies apart.

I blush again as I look at myself in the mirror. I grew up thinking anything other than traditional sex is dirty. Touching myself? Dirty. Getting myself off with one of my toys? Sinful. But the things I do with Matt? The playful seduction, him handcuffing me to his bed, blindfolding me, spanking me, controlling all of me… All offensive transgressions that will get me a place on the right hand side of Satan himself.

I splash my face with cold water, trying to cool down the flush of my cheeks that I always get when I think of Matt. The hard ridges of his body. The jagged edges of his jaw. His piercing eyes… I bite my lip and immediately splash my face once more with cold water.

"Lyric?" I jump at the soft knock on the door. "Can I come in? I'm kind of… wet. And I don't think I can make it downstairs."

I laugh as I turn and let Mariah in. Her face is a deep scarlet as she rushes into the bathroom closing the door behind her. She leans against it and stares at me wide-eyed. I smile. "Did you have fun?"

"Have you ever ridden Matt in one of those pool chairs?"

"I have not," I say as seriously as I can.

"I don't recommend it. They aren't meant for sex." She shakes her head.

I bite my cheek to stop the smile. "Good to know."

"I also don't recommend the pool deck…"

I look her up and down. It's a good thing she's already wearing barely anything. "Did you… fall in?"

"Not… entirely…" She opens the linen closet door reaching for a towel. She wraps it around her shivering body and reaches for another one to wrap around her long dark hair.

"So? What happened?"

86

"Well… we were finishing." She bites her lip. "And the next thing I know, a shadow crosses in front of the sun. I looked up just as Matt was dumping a huge, cold bucket of pool water over us."

"He…" I blink. "Did what?"

"Yeah. I didn't stutter. DJ got most of it. But apparently Matt didn't think that was enough. When DJ moved off me enough to look up at him, Matt got me with another entire bucket." She pouts.

I can't decide whether to laugh or dump a bucket of cold pool water on him in retaliation for ruining Mariah's moment. I shake my head. "I'll get him back. Somehow."

"Apparently it was in retaliation for some stupid prank DJ pulled on him."

I furrow my brows together. "What prank?"

"The last game they watched together here. I guess DJ put saran wrap on the toilet in here. Matt apparently came in here later to go to the bathroom and pissed all over the place. Apparently, it's an ongoing prank war that I got caught in the middle of."

"How childish is that?"

"It's something that's been going on for years. Years." Mariah shakes her head again and pouts more. "Anyway. Do you have anything I can change into? My clothes are still dry, but I'm not going the rest of the day with no bra or panties. Especially since it's so hot, and I'm so…" she gestures over her body. "Large chested."

I laugh. "I'm not sure I have a bra that will fit, but I can get you some panties and a sports bra."

"Thank you. I'll just be down here plotting ways to kill your boyfriend and make it look like an accident."

I laugh again as I walk out of the bathroom. DJ nearly runs me over coming up from Matt's downstairs gym. He catches me before I fall on my ass after tripping over myself to stop myself from running into him.

"Mariah okay? She was not happy when she found out the reason she got drenched."

I narrow my eyes. "Who started the prank war?"

DJ looks down at me thinking. "You know, I don't even remember. But it's been going on for a long time. I don't see it ending anytime soon."

"So both of you need to be taught a lesson. Got it."

87

"Wait. What?"

I say nothing as I head upstairs to the bedroom to get Mariah dry undergarments, but I have to chuckle as DJ calls worriedly after me. They say Brits are ruthless and cunning. All of that may be true. Maybe it isn't. What is definitely true is that we know how to get even.

A few minutes later, as the game is starting the third quarter, we all are settling in. Matt tugs me into his lap, and I realize that this is all I've ever wanted. He is all I've ever wanted.

Family.

Family is all I've ever wanted. For so long all I've had is Tyler and Brody. Now I have Matt. I have Mariah and DJ. Maybe not family by blood, but still family, and still perfect.

Chapter Ten

☆ Matt ☆

(One Week Later)

I bend down suspiciously to check my office chair. Ever since Lyric vowed revenge on me for my prank against DJ, she's managed to keep me on edge. I check every door. I check my chair for any evidence of tampering that would make me fall on my ass. I check my desk. I check drawers. At home I walk around like I'm in a fucking mine field. My eyes are on a constant swivel for anything that she might have set up to trap me. I even upturn cushions on furniture. I check my bed before I lay down.

If anyone saw the lengths I've been going through this past week, they'd think I'm fucking crazy. I might be. I don't know why such a little, submissive woman has me this far on edge. Probably because I don't know exactly the lengths she'll go to in order to get said revenge.

"What the hell are you doing?"

I jump and spin around at the voice behind me. "Fuck. DJ, don't fucking sneak up on me like that."

"Did you lose something?"

"No. Well, maybe my mind. Lyric vowed to get even with me for dousing Mariah with water during the game last week. I've been on edge the whole fucking week." I very carefully sit down in my office chair breathing a long sigh of relief when nothing happens. I don't miss the amused look DJ shoots me as he bites his lip to keep from laughing. "Shut up, you asshole."

He bursts out laughing as he starts to sit. "You realize this is all probably her plan."

"What? Watch where you sit. I haven't checked there yet."

DJ sits, not heeding my warning. Nothing happens. "She's fucking with you. Psychological warfare."

"She wouldn't do that to me. She -" I cut myself off as I think.

"Come on, man. How long have you been walking around checking everything? She's probably sitting back laughing as she watches you act like a paranoid idiot."

"Son of a bitch." I lean back in the chair. "Here I am checking everything. I look up before walking in a fucking door thinking she put a bucket of paint or some shit above the door rigged to fall on me when I walk through it."

"Psychological warfare."

"Fucking hell."

"Listen. Lyric's war against your head is the last thing on my mind. I actually have a legitimate reason for being in this office at this fucking hour when I should be home sleeping."

I look at him curiously. "You work last night?"

"Yeah. We still haven't caught Hamilton. We thought we'd get him last night, but it didn't work out. He's a slippery fucker."

I rub my eyes. "So Brody sent you in here to give me the bad news?"

"Brody went home. He was out with us last night. Dead on his feet. I told him I could handle it, but we're down a commanding officer, and we have a problem."

"I know." He doesn't need to tell me. We need to put out an alert to all officers to be on the lookout for Hamilton. We haven't been able to catch him, though we've known about several of the deals he's had selling stolen cars. If he gets away, Lyric is in more danger. The other end of the

90

coin? Lyric is about to find out I've been keeping shit from her, and she may never forgive me for that.

"We don't have a choice, Matt. I know she's going to be pissed. She's going to be pissed at me and Brody just as much. But we have to tell the team, and if we pull her from turnout, she'll be even more pissed."

"I know, DJ." I print off Hamilton's picture with a low curse under my breath. I grab the copies as I stand. "Let's get this over with. I already know the rest of my day is going to be spent begging for Lyric's forgiveness."

"She loves you."

"Yeah. I know. But I also know how much she values truth and honesty. This? This is going to break her."

"She's strong. She'll get through it." DJ stands and we both start for the turnout room. "She'll understand the reasons."

"I know she's strong. But she's about to find out that four of the five people she's let into her life betrayed her. I don't know if she'll be able to come back from that, DJ."

"Trust in your girl, Matt."

"I never should've fucking kept this from her."

"It's too late now."

I sigh as DJ and I walk to the front of the room. Lyric is sitting with Mariah. Usually when I lead a turnout and walk past her, I acknowledge her in some manner. A wink or smile. Something. Today, I keep my head down. I don't make eye contact. When I get to the front of the room, I set my stack of papers and a folder down on the podium as DJ takes his place next to me.

Before I know what's happening, there's a loud bang and glitter is raining down from the ceiling all over both me and DJ. When it settles, I blow it off my lips and wipe my hands across my face. The entire room has erupted in laughter as DJ and I look at each other.

"I was wrong. Psychological warfare and fucking vindictive British Queen of Pranks. I bow down to you, Your Excellence," DJ says loud enough for a laughing Lyric to hear.

Lyric stands up on the turnout table. "Bow! Bow down to your Queen!" The officers in the room teasingly bow.

After a few minutes of letting them laugh it up and unwind, and after DJ and I get as much glitter off us as we can, I open my folder.

91

"Listen up!" I say above the din. Everyone quiets almost immediately. My heart jumps into my throat. I know I need to do this, but I feel like I'm about to lose the best thing that's ever happened to me. I clear my throat. "Over the past few weeks, we've seen an uptick in car thefts of luxury cars. Some of you are aware of this because you've been on the task force. Others aren't." I avoid Lyric's eyes at all costs.

"In my hand, I have an image of the person we've discovered is leading the entire ring," DJ jumps in. "Thanks to Ms. Sharpe's antics, you all now get to share in the glitter." I silently thank DJ for trying to ease the blow Lyric is about to feel.

I take a deep breath. "The leader's name is..." I can't stop myself from meeting my girl's eyes, wondering if it's the last time she'll let me look in them. "Hamilton Prescott." I don't take my eyes off hers. She's all I see. The hurt and betrayal that fills her beautiful features cuts me to the core. But I have to continue. "Prescott is from the United Kingdom. He's an ex-cop. We've been working with an officer in the UK. He's given us documentation that Prescott has been leading this ring for several years. He moved to the United States a few years ago now, but it looks like all of his efforts have been here for the past two years."

Lyric gasps as she looks at me. She puts her hand to her mouth. I can see the tears. "How?"

Several people look back at her. To keep the attention off her, I continue. "Eyes forward," I command. All attention is back on me. I look down at my paperwork to regain my composure before looking back up, my attention solely on her. "For the past few weeks we've had a task force in place led by Sergeant Rens and Captain Brody McKay. This task force has been keeping tabs on this ring. They've tried to bust them. A couple have been caught, but Prescott has managed to get away." I swallow. The hurt in her eyes is stifling.

DJ catches my eye as he walks back up the aisle. "As the leader of this task force, it's my duty to keep you all informed. Prescott is considered dangerous. Deranged even. I won't give names, but there is some involvement with one of our own. Which means this case hits close to home." DJ turns and faces everyone. "I don't think I need to tell you what that means. This guy is top priority."

There's a chorus of whispers throughout the room as what DJ said sinks in. They probably all know who the officer involved is. We don't need to say a word. To a cop, it really doesn't matter who it is. If they're aware it's one of their partners, they'll all form an impenetrable blue line of protection around that officer. Judging from the looks I'm getting from Lyric, I'm thanking all of the Gods for that because she may never let me near her again.

"Now get out there. Get this guy. Find him. And when you do, call it out. You'll have everyone out there rushing to you for backup," I finish as I dismiss everyone. DJ remains at my side. Mariah stays at Lyric's. When everyone is out of the room, Lyric stands leveling me with the most intense glare I've ever seen.

"How could you keep this from me? How could you know about this and not tell me? I've been out there each and every shift thinking he could jump out at me from anywhere. Scared out of my mind. And here you guys are watching his every move!"

"Lyric. It's not like that, baby," I plead. I never fucking plead. With anyone. For any reason. My chest is so tight I can hardly breathe.

Mariah stands next to her, putting a hand on her arm. "Maybe you should at least hear him out," she says softly as DJ and I start making our way towards her.

Lyric rips her arm away, glaring at Mariah. "Don't touch me."

Mariah bites her lip and steps back into DJ's arms just as DJ and I reach them. "Lyric, Mariah didn't know," DJ says.

"You tell her everything!" she cries. Tears fill her eyes. "Everything! And you left me completely out of it. I'm the one he's after! Not you! Not any of you!" She turns and sobs as she flees the room. Mariah turns and buries her face in DJ's chest.

I don't hesitate in running after Lyric. "Lyric! Stop." She doesn't. I didn't expect her to. I speed up and catch her just as she passes my office door. I pull her inside and shut the door, standing in front of it so she can't leave. "Lyric. Please just listen to me."

"Listen to you? Are you out of your mind?" She's shrieking at me, and I can do nothing but let her. "You kept such a huge thing from me! How can I trust you? How can I ever trust you again?" She tries to shove past me, but I catch her around the waist and hold her to me. She shoves against me. Realizing she's not getting out of my grasp, she starts pounding on my chest. "Let go! Let me go!"

93

She's crying and screaming at me, but I hold her tighter until she's so weak from crying and screaming and hitting me that she collapses. I bring us both to our knees as I hug her. She curls up into me, gripping my shirt in her fists tightly as she sobs, gasping for air. She buries her face in my chest and trembles.

"I'm sorry. I'm so sorry, baby," I whisper into her hair as I rock with her. "I should've told you. I kept it from you because I wanted to protect you. I didn't want you to have to deal with it. None of us did."

"I feel like you all… betrayed me…" She hiccups against me as she tries to catch her breath.

"Baby, DJ wasn't lying to you. Mariah had nothing to do with it. She didn't know about the taskforce. We kept it lowkey. He kept it from her because he knew she'd tell you. But it wasn't all because of you. We felt like we could catch him quickly. None of us believed that he would elude us. We were wrong. We do think that since he hasn't been calling you or leaving you packages anywhere that his focus is on staying out of our grasp. So the task force wasn't a total failure. It kept his attention off you."

"I don't have very many people in my life I can count on. Other than my nana, I've never allowed anyone close to me. Except Tyler. And then Brody. It took me a long time to really trust Mariah enough to open up to her about the things I did tell her. And DJ. But you. Matt. I let you in so far and so deep. Faster than anyone. I fell so in love with you in such a record amount of time… This hurts. It hurts me that you kept this from me. That all of you did."

"I know. It was wrong. I should've told you. I'm sorry, baby." I tangle my fingers in her hair and kiss her neck and side of her head. "Lyric, I know how hurt you are. And I understand why. I know you're upset. I know asking for your forgiveness right now is a far-fetched request. But I need you to know that I love you. More than I can ever put into words. I need you in my life. I don't know what I'd do without you. I know you need time. But please don't leave me. I'd never survive it."

She looks up at me, wiping her eyes. "Matt…"

I feel a tear slide down my cheek. I don't remember the last time I cried. I'm not entirely sure I've ever cried. Another tear falls. "Lyric, I've never in my life felt so intensely for anyone. You fit with me. I know I fit with you. I know you're mad, and I know you need time. Just please don't leave. I've never begged or pleaded for anything, but I'll get on my knees for you and beg and plead if that's what it takes."

She reaches up and wipes away my tears with the pad of her thumb. "Matt. Yes, I'm hurt. And upset. But I'm not going anywhere. I can't envision my life without you in it," she says raspily.

She collapses against me. I collapse in relief against the door and hold her closely. "I'm sorry, Lyric. I'm really sorry."

"Please, please don't keep anything like this from me again. I… can't… deal with that." She shakes her head. "I can't."

"I won't. I know how wrong it was. I thought I was protecting you, but the truth is, you need to know what's happening. You need to be aware so you can be vigilant. So you aren't blindsided, and so you're able to feel like you have the tools to protect yourself. I want to be your soldier, but a soldier is only as good as the team he has behind him. You're part of my team. I can't treat you like a helpless woman who needs me to save her. That's not what you are. That's never been what you are."

She sniffles. "I need to apologize to Mariah… And I think I need to talk to DJ and Brody. And probably Tyler."

I can't help but chuckle a little. "Should I clear out the station so you can scream and yell at them?"

"I was really mean," she breathes into my chest.

"Don't. Don't apologize. We all deserve it. The only one you need to apologize to is Mariah. She didn't know about the taskforce. DJ was under strict orders to say nothing to her."

"So, she didn't know… She would've said something if she had…"

"Exactly." She shifts and takes a deep breath as she stands. I follow but lead her to a chair. "Stay here. Compose yourself. I'll bring them here. We can do a conference call with Brody and Tyler."

I watch as she gratefully sinks into one of my office chairs. I quickly find DJ and Mariah still huddled in the turnout room. Mariah is tucked protectively in DJ's arms as they stand swaying quietly together.

"It's okay, baby. She'll realize you had nothing to do with it soon," DJ says to her as he kisses the top of her head.

"You didn't see the way she looked at me…," Mariah says miserably.

"Mariah, it was my fault," I say next to her. "It was my fault, and I already owned up to it. She wants to talk. She's in my office. She knows you weren't involved and wants to apologize."

She looks up at me with bloodshot owl eyes. "She... does?"

"She was hurt. She's okay. But she'd like to talk to us. I think everyone needs to hear her out."

Mariah nods and DJ takes her hand. They both follow me back to my office. I enter first with DJ behind me. Lyric keeps her eyes low. DJ gently tugs Mariah in behind him. She looks at the floor and stays close to his back. Lyric leaps up as I close the door and hugs Mariah, burying her face in her hair.

"I'm so sorry! I was so hurt, and I thought since DJ tells you everything, that he told you and that you all kept it from me! I felt so alone..."

Mariah turns and hugs her so tightly, I question if she might break her. "I would never, never have let them keep it from you if I knew."

"It's why we didn't tell her, honey," I say as I sit down behind my desk to get Brody and Tyler on the phone. I watch as my girl and Mariah grip each other as tightly as they can.

A few minutes later I have both Brody and Tyler on speaker phone. DJ is perched on the edge of my desk. Mariah is holding Lyric's hand. I smile knowing what's coming. Something about my girl sticking up for herself and facing down all of us is hot as fuck.

Lyric takes a deep breath. "So... I've gathered you all here today because of this taskforce you've put together, and you stupidly not informing me of. I'm not a little girl. I'm not a damsel in distress. I'm not saying that I can go up against him on my own. I'm not stupid. I know how foolish that would be. But keeping this from me wasn't right. I felt betrayed. I felt... completely alone. I know why you did it. And I'm grateful. But I also know that you all know I'm not the type of woman who wants everything done for her. I felt powerless. I became a cop so I could feel independent and help people when they need it. So I never had to feel powerless again. You effectively took that from me, and it hurt."

"Lyric, hurting you was never our intention," Tyler says. "The intention has always been to protect you and keep Hamilton away from you."

"But not by taking me completely out of the situation, Tyler. You of all people know how hurtful that is. Keeping me in the dark about something that concerns me and my safety isn't fair to me."

"Lyric, we thought we could catch him. Just get him out of your hair," DJ says.

"But you didn't. According to both of you, this has been ongoing."

"We were in too deep by the time we all realized we should've told you," Brody chips in.

"I would have preferred you had told me rather than me learning about it in front of the department."

"She's right," I say before anyone else says another word. "We fucked up. From now on, Lyric stays informed of everything. She may feel safe with me, but she has a right to know everything that's happening. None of us in this room or on the phone would feel totally safe if we were kept in the dark like she was. No matter how much we trust those around us."

Everyone agrees as Lyric shoots me a grateful smile. Mariah rubs the back of her hand with her thumb and wipes away a tear from her own eye. DJ leans forward and hugs Lyric, whispering something in her ear that makes her giggle.

And just like that I have my girl back. After coming so close to losing her, I vow to myself that I'll never let that happen again. She's become my whole world. Just like I won't let anything hurt her, I won't risk anything that could take her away from me.

Lyric Sharpe is my universe.

Chapter Eleven

☆ Lyric ☆

(Two Weeks Later)

A couple of weeks after my heart to heart with my family, Matt and I are parked in a parking lot near the edge of town. I'm stretching over the hood of the squad car as the afternoon sun beats down on me. I yawn and adjust my sunglasses before bending and stretching over the hood of the squad again.

"Do you have any idea how much I want to fuck you right now?" He's looking down at his phone as he leans against the door.

I freeze and look up at Matt through my lashes. I bite my lip as I straighten. "Sorry."

He looks over at me. "Well, don't stop." He gives me a sexy lopsided grin. I blush a deep shade of red but obey and go back to stretching. He goes back to his phone.

"So, why are we here? You still haven't told me."

"There's supposed to be a deal going down around here."

"Aren't we a little out in the open?" I extend a leg behind me and hold the position for a few moments before switching and doing the other one.

"If the deal were going on up here." He gives me the same sexy smile he just had but doesn't look at me.

I look around, tilting my head, before my eyes land on the overpass. "Do you mean… underneath the overpass?" I look at him curiously.

He nods. "He plans on doing it in the park. Lots of people."

I look at him incredulously. "He's going to sell a stolen car in broad daylight in the middle of a busy park?"

"Yep. Brazen son of a bitch."

"When?" My heart races, but I force it to steady. I lean against the car next to Matt. He shows me his phone. "Five. So…, an hour?"

"That's what we think. But so far, he's always been earlier. It's like he tells people a time and shows up earlier to scope the place out. He's smart. But we think we've managed to outsmart him this time. Our job is to stay up here. If he flees up here, we'll catch him. We have all the exits blocked. We have the park surrounded with unmarked and undercover officers from our department as well as county and state."

"So you think we'll get him this time?"

"We'll get him. In the meantime…" He straightens and looks around. He puts his radio on top of the roof of the car before slowly turning me around.

"What are you doing?" I ask him suspiciously.

He runs his hands up my thighs to my hips. He kisses my neck and up to my ear. "Haven't you learned by now that you should trust me and not question me?" I feel his unmistakable hard as steel dick pressed against my ass as he works to unbuckle my duty belt before he reaches for the button on my uniform pants. As soon as it's undone, my pants slide down. He spreads my legs before my pants hit the ground so that they stop at my knees.

I tilt my head to the side to give him more access as he kisses my neck. Two of his long, made-for-finger-fucking fingers thrust hard into my pussy. "Fuck! Matt!"

"Shh! You want people to hear?" he growls dominantly against my neck.

99

"No…," I whisper breathlessly as he thrusts hard and fast, keeping me pressed against the car.

"No, what?"

"No, sir," I say, submitting instantly to him. I place my hands on top of the car. I've learned that he likes when my hands are wrapped around him or tied or cuffed to something when he's doing anything sexual with me. Since all I want to do is please him, I'm happy to oblige.

"Good girl." He rubs his dick firmly against my ass and holds me to him with one of his perfectly well-built arms while his fingers bring me closer and closer to the euphoria he always brings to me.

I bite my arm and pant as I ride his fingers. He starts rubbing my clit, and I nearly cry with the state of bliss I'm in. "Ah!" I scream into my arm when he flicks it back and forth. My pussy clenches hard and starts pulsing. The pulses feel like they're vibrating in waves throughout my body. "Matt! Please! Please!"

He chuckles against my shoulder and keeps thrusting hard and fast. He spreads his fingers inside me and keeps rubbing my clit at the same furious pace he's ramming his fingers into my pussy. "Please, what?"

"Please, sir! Please, let me come!" I'm so close to rocketing onto another plain. I dig my nails into the roof and push back against him.

"Come for me, pretty girl."

"Oh, God." I try to stay quiet as I clench around him. I come so hard, I jerk hard into the squad.

He pushes harder against me, thrusting me through it with a low growl. "Good girl. So beautiful when you come for me."

I whimper as he slows even further, helping my pulsating pussy come down from such an intense orgasm. "Fuck… Matt." I pant shakily, my body suddenly feeling languid. Matt holds me steady, his fingers still deep inside me, as I come down. After a few moments, he slowly pulls out of me and takes a step back, keeping me shielded from anyone's view but his. I reach down and pull my pants up. I turn to him as I button everything. He's sucking me off his fingers with a satisfied smile. I blush. "Why is that so hot?"

"Because you like watching me enjoy you."

I shudder as I situate my uniform. Over his shoulder I catch a glimpse of movement in the woods. I tilt my head. Matt watches me curiously and starts to turn. I grab his shirt, my eyes staying where I saw the movement.

"Don't turn around," I whisper. "But I think someone is in the woods."

Matt nods. "Follow my lead. Understand?" I meet his eyes and nod almost imperceptibly. My eyes dart back to the woods. Matt leans down to kiss me, pulling me close to him. "Keep your eyes on the woods," he says against my lips.

He stands back up and turns, maneuvering me behind him, but not all the way. He pushes me back against the car and leans against me, his arm across me and his hand on my hip. He takes off his sunglasses and inspects them.

I kiss his arm, speaking against it softly. "What are you doing?"

He puts his sunglasses back on. "Acting like we have no idea anyone is out there."

I shiver next to him. "We're exposed. What if he has a gun?"

"He had more than enough of an opportunity to use it when my fingers were buried in your pussy. Are you sure it's a guy?"

"I just caught a glimpse of his jacket. It was white."

He blinks a couple times. "White."

"Yeah. It reminded me of the suit jacket Hamilton wore on the date we went on."

"You think it was him?"

"How many guys do you know as cocky as he is who would wear a white jacket when he's spying, and trying to hide in the woods?"

"Point taken. Stay here."

I look up at him. "What?"

"Stay. Here. If it was him, and he runs out of the woods, we need someone here to catch him. I'll have DJ meet you here. Won't take him long. He's across the street."

I grab his arm. Not out of fear for myself. Out of fear for him. Paralyzing fear. "Matt. Don't. You need backup. Wait for DJ. Please? He can go with you. Or I can. Please?"

"Lyric. Baby, I've seen his pictures. He's no match for me."

I can tell my eyes are getting wilder because I'm picturing so many different scenarios and none of them are ones that he makes it out alive. "Matt…"

He leans down and kisses me again before he grabs his radio. "SWAT One to SWAT Three."

"SWAT Three."

"My location. Pronto."

"On my way. Less than a minute."

Matt clips his radio to his belt. "Stay here. I mean it, Lyric."

I chew on the inside of my cheek. "Matt. Please be careful."

"I promise." He takes out his gun and heads for the woods. He uses the trees for cover as he walks deeper and deeper into the wooded area. Like a flash, I see a blur of a white jacket take off in the opposite direction of Matt, further towards the outskirts of the city. I don't need to look behind me to know that DJ is pulling into the lot.

I act on instinct and adrenaline. I know if he gets away, this game of cat and mouse he's playing with me will never end. I refuse to live my life in fear of him and what his deranged mind will come up with next to torture me. I take off after him.

"Nine-Forty-Two in foot pursuit!" I yell into my radio. I don't technically have a squad today. When that happens, we use badge numbers. "Suspect is running Northwest from my location!" I pump my legs as fast as I can keeping him in my line of sight.

"Lyric! Stop!" DJ yells after me. I can hear him behind me, but if I stop, Hamilton will get away. He's already really far ahead of me.

I run faster.

"SWAT One to Nine-Forty-Two. What the hell are you doing?" Matt's deep voice comes over my radio, and he sounds pissed. But I don't stop. I can't.

I leap over a tree branch as Hamilton stumbles and nearly falls over something. He recovers and looks behind him. Up until this point, I only had a feeling that it was Hamilton. Instinct. But now I know. His sickeningly aristocratic features. His rat-like eyes. His porcelain doll nose. His mousy, runt-like body. It's like he's a spaghetti noodle flailing in the wind.

But it's the look in his eyes that has me swallowing. The hatred. All directed towards me. Like I'm the reason for all of his life-problems. Maybe I am. Maybe I broke him somehow. Or maybe he's just all kinds of crazy and deserves to be locked up in a mental institution. Maybe I need to call Batman. Have him come take him to Gotham City and lock him up in Arkham Asylum with all the other psychotic supervillain wannabes.

"Dammit, Lyric! Stop!" DJ yells.

I don't look back. "I can't!" I'm running as hard as I can, getting a little out of breath.

"Lyric! That's a fucking order! Stop!" DJ yells. In response, I run harder. I'm finally gaining ground on Hamilton.

"Lyric! Stop pursuit!" Matt yells. He's running with DJ now.

"I've almost got him!" I yell back as Hamilton dodges to his right. "He's heading Northeast! Right towards County One!"

"Fuck! Lyric, I said stop!" Matt yells. "That's a direct order from your commanding officer!"

Hamilton runs across a small rickety bridge that collapses under his feet. It spans across a narrow ravine with a small creek flowing underneath. He makes it to the other side unscathed. I gage the jump, not slowing down. Hamilton smirks over his shoulder, probably thinking I'm not going to follow. It's only about six feet. If I run hard enough and fast enough, I know I can make it.

"Lyric! Fucking stop! Now!" DJ screams behind me. I can hear him getting closer. Another set of footsteps pounds the ground with his.

"God fucking dammit, Lyric. Stop!" Matt yells.

"I can't! I'll lose him!"

"Don't you dare fucking jump!" Matt commands.

I shake my head, keeping my eyes on Hamilton. His eyes widen when he realizes I'm not stopping. I leap over the ravine, praying to every God that exists or doesn't that I make it. Hamilton takes off running again, switching his direction. I hit the edge and feel myself sliding backwards.

"Ah!" I scream. I pitch forward and propel myself, hitting my knees on the ground.

"Lyric!" Matt and DJ both yell in unison.

I take a deep breath and quickly get up, chasing after Hamilton again. "Suspect heading due North!" I call into my radio. I glance back and see both Matt and DJ easily making the jump. I know how pissed they both are at me, but I feel so much better knowing they are close.

"Lyric! I swear to fuck I'll suspend you!" Matt yells.

"Fuck that! I'll have you fired for disobeying your commanding officers! Fucking stop!" DJ orders.

Hamilton disappears over a small hill.

I don't stop. I follow him, cresting the hill in seconds. I'm close enough that if I leap, I can tackle him to the ground.

I don't think.

I act.

I jump and land on his back, knocking him hard on the ground.

"Ah!" he screams as he hits.

"Stay down! Don't move!" I recover quickly and drop my knee between his shoulder blades.

"Get off!" He flails, but I don't let up.

"Hands behind your back!"

"Get off!"

"Get your hands behind your back!"

"Fuck you! Get the fuck off!" He bucks wildly. I drop my knee harder between his shoulder blades until he quits struggling. I let up on the pressure, but don't allow him to move.

"Get your hands behind your back right now!" I command.

"Lyric! Fucking hell!" Matt says as he drops to my side. DJ drops to the other side and both of them wrestle Hamilton's hands behind his back. They cuff him quickly. I stand and back away slightly to catch my breath as they haul him to his feet.

"You're fucking fired. Do you understand me?" DJ glares at me. It's only then that the entire last few minutes play back in my head.

"I..." I blink as if I'm coming out of an adrenaline induced dream world and take another step back. I disobeyed both DJ and Matt. My commanding officers. All I was thinking about was getting Hamilton. But they both told me to back off. I disobeyed.

Matt glares down at me as other officers start showing up. "You're suspended. Pending an investigation into your actions. Disobeying commanding officers is a fucking no go." He grabs my upper arm and yanks me away from Hamilton and the other officers. I look down, afraid to see the disappointment I can feel radiating from his eyes. "And furthermore, you disobeyed your fucking dominant. But worse than that? You disobeyed your boyfriend. The one person in this fucking world who wants nothing more than for you to be safe. Do you think I was telling you to stop for the fun of it?"

I shake my head. "No..."

"Go home. Now."

I shiver and look around. "I don't really know how to get out of here," I whisper.

"Fuck me. DJ!"

"Yeah, boss?"

Matt lets go of my arm and starts to walk towards Hamilton. "Take her home."

My heart feels like it's literally shattering. It hurts to breathe. "Matt!" I start to follow him, but DJ catches me. Matt doesn't turn around.

I gasp, my lungs burning like they aren't getting air. Tears immediately start falling at the thought that he's walking away.

For good.

That I messed up so badly that he hates me.

That he doesn't want me anymore.

DJ grabs my hand and starts to lead me out of the woods. I start crying, unable to stop. DJ is talking, but I can't hear him. I don't care what he's saying anyway. All I care about is that I disappointed Matt. I hurt him. I don't care about my job. I don't care about Hamilton.

All I care about is that Matt walked away. He didn't even turn back to look at me. It was like he was just done. I made him so angry that he just decided he'd had enough of me. That I don't warrant his love. The realization that he's right, that I don't deserve him, crushes me.

And it's a blow I know I'll never recover from.

Chapter Twelve

☆ Matt ☆

I don't know what time it is when we finally clear the scene and finish the paperwork that goes along with it, but when I finally walk into my house, I'm fucking exhausted. It's not just because of the work Hamilton Prescott created. I'm exhausted because the adrenaline rush I got long ago evaporated. The one that started when I was terrified for the life of my girl. I feel like I crash landed a long time ago. All I want now is to wrap myself around Lyric and convince myself that she's okay.

What I walk into, though, has my heart both racing and faltering at the same time. The house is completely dark. Whenever I have a SWAT call or I'm running late, Lyric leaves a light on. She can't sleep without me so she's usually laying on the couch with the TV on. The TV is off. She's not on the couch. The throw blanket I leave for her is still neatly spread over the back of the couch.

That fear I felt earlier comes thundering back to me, slamming into me with a force that sends me reeling. "Lyric!" I call out. I check all of the rooms downstairs. I check by the pool. I check in the pool. I run upstairs, crashing through the bedroom door. "Lyric!" I check the bathroom. The balcony. Panic sets in, and I start questioning if Hamilton had accomplices. If maybe someone he was working with took her.

I look around the room for any clue that might lead me to where she is. "Lyric!" The closet door is slightly ajar so I run to it, throwing it open with such force that the door comes off the hinges. It takes me a moment to realize that all of her stuff is gone. I stagger backwards until the back of my knees hit the bed. I sit staring at the closet. My heart beats so fast I'm positive it can be heard next door.

I shake my head and reach shakily to the drawer of the nightstand. I open it to find it empty. All of the toys I took so much pleasure in teasing her with are gone. The teddy bear, the only thing she had been able to salvage from her home before it had been burned to the ground, is gone. It was one of the only things she had left of her grandmother.

Trembling, I walk to the dresser. I'd given her the top two drawers. I intended to get her her own dresser so she didn't have to stuff all of her things in the two drawers and hang things she wasn't used to hanging because she didn't have room in the dresser to put them. Everything in her drawers is gone.

Dazed, I walk down the stairs. The little things that made this house just as much Lyric's as mine have disappeared. The silk purple lilies in the silver vase by the front door aren't there. The black Gainesville SWAT hoodie I always find Lyric wearing is neatly folded on the arm of the oversized chair she loves to read in.

I drop to my knees in the middle of the living room and take out my phone. I dial her number, but she doesn't answer. The sweet voice message she had has been turned to a dreary computer telling me to leave a message at the beep. I get dizzy. The room starts spinning at warp speed. I close my eyes, but it only gets worse. I crash to my ass with my back against the chair and swallow down the bile rising from my stomach. It's like I'm experiencing the worst hangover of my life.

I don't know how I do it, but I manage to call DJ. I bring the phone shakily to my ear waiting for him to answer. I don't know if my heart has stopped beating, or if it's beating so fast I can't feel it anymore, but I start gasping for air.

"Lieutenant."

"DJ." I cough as I sputter.

"Matt? What the fuck? Are you okay?"

107

"She's gone. She… she left." I clutch my chest and grunt. I feel like I'm having a heart attack.

"What do you mean she left? I dropped her off at your house. She told me she needed time alone. Said she'd call Mariah in a while."

"She took everything. All her stuff." I clutch my chest harder and groan through the pain.

"Matt, are you okay? What's happening? You sound like you're in pain."

"I need to find Lyric, DJ," I whisper, knowing she's the only thing that can cure the heartbreak.

"Mariah!" DJ calls. "Where's Lyric?" I shift and sit up straighter still rubbing my aching chest. "What the fuck do you mean you don't know?"

"Fuck…" I force myself up. My knees nearly buckle, but I fight through it. I have to get to her.

"Mariah hasn't heard from her, Matt." I can hear the concern in his voice as I drag myself to the door.

"Let me know." I hang up, not waiting for a response. There's only one other person I know to call. Brody. I dial his number as I pull myself weakly into my truck. I start it and begin backing out of my driveway, praying for him to answer.

"Matthew."

"You know I hate being called Matthew."

"And you know how I feel about Lyric. She's like my little girl."

"She's gone, Brody. She took everything. Please tell me where she is." I start driving towards his house. "Is she with you?"

"No. She's not with me."

The pain in my chest feels like a dagger through my heart. "Brody. Please tell me where my girl is."

"Your girl? She's not exactly feeling like your girl right now. Not after you walked away from her in her most vulnerable time. She needed you. At least reassurance that you'd fucking see her at home."

Everything that happened earlier hits me like a hundred mile an hour baseball to the head. I was pissed that she disobeyed. I was terrified she was going to get herself hurt, so I dealt with it by letting my anger at her blatant insubordination take over.

I walked away.

I did the one thing I vowed to her I'd never do.

"Fuck. Fuck! Brody, I have to fix this. Please tell me where she is. Did she go back to her apartment?"

"No. Against my advice, she asked me to drop her off at the airport. I couldn't talk her out of it. She's getting on a flight to the United Kingdom. Actually… I'm watching the plane take off right now. She's gone, Matt. And there's not a fucking thing I could do about it. You really fucked her up. I don't know if she'll ever be able to come back from this."

I step hard on the gas and fly through the streets towards Gainesville International Airport. "I'll get her back."

"Yeah? How do you plan on doing that? Growing a pair of wings and chasing after her? Stealing a jet?" I can hear how hurt he is, and I know I'm the cause of it. "You'd do best to stay the fuck away from her. I mean it, Matt. I see your truck anywhere near here, I'm kicking your fucking ass. Got me?"

"Brody, I know you're mad. I deserve it. But there's no one who's going to stop me from going after her. Not you. Not Tyler. No one." I hang up the phone as I reach the airport. I come to a skidding stop in a fire lane and jump out.

"Hey! You can't park there!" an airport security guard says.

I toss him my keys as I run to the door. "Tow it!" I run to the ticket desk. The sleepy woman behind the counter startles when I slam my wallet on the counter. "Get me a ticket to London."

She looks up at me, a hint of fear in her eyes as they flick towards the security officer near the security check-in line. She clears her throat. "Yes, sir." She starts tapping on keys. "I have one seat left on the flight for tomorrow afternoon. Otherwise, there's a seat on the next flight that leaves in thirty minutes, but it's first class. The ticket is nearly a thousand dollars." She looks up at me hesitantly.

"I don't fucking care. Book it." I toss my driver's license down on the counter and passport card. She breathes a sigh of relief as she starts booking my flight. Moments later, she hands me my ticket. I quickly run for the security check-in, thankful there's no line. It doesn't take long to get through since I have no baggage. I make my way quickly to the gate just as boarding begins.

"Enjoy your flight," the young kid says as he scans my ticket. I say nothing as I walk down the walkway to get to the plane. I board, find my seat quickly, and sit.

I mentally curse myself as I look out the window. How the fuck I could do what I did to her knowing everything she's been through is something I'll never understand. How I could ignore her when she called my name after I turned away is a mistake that I'll never be able to forgive myself for. Especially if it's what costs me my relationship with Lyric. She's the only woman I've ever loved. I'll be damned if I give her up without a fight.

✮✮✮

A very long eleven hours, and a fuck of a lot of turbulence later, I stumble off the plane convinced that if my stomach hadn't already been in my mouth, it would have relocated there after that. I scrub my hands across my face and head for the nearest bathroom, stopping at a small shop on my way. I brought nothing with me. I need to clean up. I smell like sweat and dirt from the chase yesterday. At least I think it was yesterday. I didn't sleep on the plane. For all I know it's still yesterday. Or today.

Fuck.

I yawn as I head for the bathroom to clean up as much as I can. At least enough to make myself seem human. Not a crazed psychotic maniac chasing his girl halfway across the world to apologize for all of his sins.

My stomach growls, and I groan. I haven't eaten anything since yesterday when I was sitting at my desk doing paperwork. I don't think I've had anything to drink either. I briefly play with the idea of ignoring all of it and immediately calling Tyler.

The truth is that I can't do that. As much as I would love to find Lyric right now and bring her home, I know that I have to feed myself. I'd much rather take her in my arms and beg for forgiveness than fall at her feet, weak from lack of sleep and nourishment. I know I need the food as much as I need the few minutes I took to freshen up.

I make my way out of the bathroom and to a coffee shop to grab a quick bite and a cup of coffee. I sit at a table and compose my thoughts. They've been all over the place the entire flight. I can't walk up to Lyric

110

and start babbling a bunch of incoherent words. She deserves me at my best when I grovel.

When I'm finished, I clean up my mess and head for the exit, but I'm slowed down by a group of passengers getting off a flight from somewhere. I maneuver my way through the throngs of chaos when I'm bumped from behind. Unable to stop myself, I crash into the back of the tiny woman in front of me. She falls over her suitcase and lands hard on the floor with a whimper.

"Shit…," she whimpers.

"Fuck. I'm sorry. I couldn't catch myself in time." I kneel down next to her, but she's become completely frozen. I gingerly put my hand on her arm. "Ma'am? Are you okay?"

Very slowly, she turns to me, her dark hair a mess and covering her face. I get a whiff of Lyric's soft and subtle vanilla bean scent. My heart skips a beat. With an unsteady hand, I hesitantly push her hair behind her ear as people hurry around us, not stopping for anything. When her beautiful eyes meet mine, shining with unshed tears, I lose it. I drop fully to my knees and pull her into me, crying like a little boy into her hair, and not giving two shits who sees.

I don't know how long we stay in the middle of the busy walkway, trembling against each other and rocking our bodies as we hold each other, but I eventually come back to myself and realize that we need to move. Saying nothing, I pull her up with me. I reach down for her carry-on, not taking my arm away from her waist, and then pull her to an empty waiting area.

After we're settled, I cup her chin and lift it so she's looking at me, but she refuses to look in my eyes. "Lyric," I choke out over the lump in my throat.

"What are you doing here?" she whispers.

"What? Baby, why wouldn't I be here? Did you think I was going to let you walk out of my life like that?"

"I thought you didn't want me anymore." She deflates and starts crying again.

I pull her close, hugging her as tightly as possible. "I will never not want you. You mean fucking everything to me."

"But… you… walked… away!" Her body trembles against me as she grips the waistband of my jeans.

"I was angry that you didn't listen, Lyric. I was scared to death you were going to get hurt, and I covered that fear over with anger so I didn't panic. I walked away because I needed to calm down. I would never walk away from you. Never."

"You..." She sniffles and burrows into me. "Were scared?"

"I was terrified," I breathe into her neck. I run my hands up and down her back. "All I could think about was him turning around and shooting, or him disappearing and grabbing you. When you jumped over the creek and slipped, I thought that was it. I thought you were down. But when you disappeared over that hill..." My grip on her tightens, and I take a deep breath.

"I'm sorry..."

I shake my head. "No. Don't. You don't have anything to be sorry for. I didn't handle it right. I didn't handle any of that right, and I almost lost you because of it."

"I could handle you being upset... But when you walked away... And ignored me when I called your name... I... thought -"

"I know, baby. I'm so fucking sorry. I didn't think you'd take it like that. I thought you'd go home, and we'd talk about what happened when I got there. But when I got home, and you were gone..." I run my fingers through her hair and tug it a little. "Fuck, Lyric, I thought I was going to die. That's no exaggeration. I felt like I was having a heart attack at the thought of losing you."

She pulls away enough to look up at me. Her eyes are wide. She rests her hand over my heart while the other one firmly grips my waistband. "Are you okay? I'm sorry, Matt! I didn't think you loved me anymore. I -"

I cut her off with a deep kiss and low moan. She instantly submits to me, just like she always does, and it's then I know for certain that I haven't lost her. That she's still mine. I don't pull back until we both stop trembling.

"Lyric. I love you. More than anything. I don't want you to ever think that I don't want you or love you. Even if I walk away for a minute if I'm angry, I'll never walk away from you. I'll always come back to you." I gesture outside the terminal window. "This isn't your home anymore. Your home is with me. It's always going to be with me." I put my hands on both sides of her face and run both thumbs under her eyes to wipe away her tears.

She closes her eyes and melts into me. "I'm sorry I ran. I… just didn't think you wanted me anymore." She opens her eyes. "I fell so hard for you. I felt like I lost you, and it cut me open. I just didn't feel like there was anything there for me without you. I had Mariah and DJ and Brody, but seeing you everyday and knowing how upset and disappointed you were. And then knowing DJ was just as disappointed and angry at me for disobeying you both. I knew Brody would be upset. And I know how much Mariah believes in rules and safety. I really thought you all would hate me."

"Honey, that's never going to happen. Never. Do you understand me? Mariah and DJ are like the family you never had. So is Brody. You've told me that. Families fight. Fuck, they might even scream and yell, but none of us are ever going to leave you. We're not walking away. If I hadn't come here, you know Mariah would have killed me, and then been on the next flight to drag you home."

She chuckles a little, and I smile, grateful to get at least that out of her. "She's really going to be mad that I left like that."

"No. She is going to be grateful when you come home, though."

She smiles softly before burrowing back into me. "I'm sorry I left."

"Don't. Just please come home. Your family loves you. I love you. We can't live without you, baby. Don't make us." I kiss the top of her head and tangle my fingers in her hair. "Come home, Lyric. Come home where you belong."

She nods into my chest. "I'll come home."

I feel like a giant weight has been lifted off my shoulders. Hearing those words… I can breathe. "Thank God. Thank God, baby. I don't know what I would have done if you'd said no."

"Probably throw me over your shoulder and haul me back caveman style."

I can't help but laugh, thankful that she's got a little of her sass back. "You forgot the part where I spank you for blatantly disobeying and leaving me with no word." I smile into her and kiss her neck as I close my eyes, breathing her sweet scent in.

"I think I might like that…"

"Fuck, Lyric, where have you been all my life?"

She giggles and looks up at me. She kisses my jaw. "Let's go home."

"Gladly." I pull her up and grab her carry-on.

After we grab her bags, I take her hand and head straight for a gate. Any gate that will get us on a plane home.

Home.

Where I can show my girl just where she belongs so she never questions her place in my life again.

Chapter Thirteen

★ Lyric ★

(Two Months Later)

I'm starting to enjoy lazy days off more and more the longer I'm with Matt. After he chased after me and brought me home from London, I almost immediately moved in with him. And the past couple of months have been heavenly.

Sitting on the pool chair in the sun reading while he fiddles around the house fixing random things that may or may not need to be fixed has become one of my favorite things to do. I enjoy reading. And the view of his muscles glistening in the sun isn't bad.

I bite my lip as I get to a particularly sexy part of my book. The main characters are just about to get a little hot against a wall. I swing my feet in the air as I lay on my stomach, enjoying the sun beating down on my back.

Just as I get to their climax, a hand comes down hard on my ass. "Hey!"

Matt sits down on the chair next to me and takes my Kindle before I have a chance to say or do anything. He smirks as he reads. "He rubs my slick nub." He laughs. "What the fuck are you reading?"

I pout up at him. "I happen to like that…"

"Spank me harder!" He laughs harder. "You have to be kidding me with this."

"Okay. The sex scenes are admittedly a little…" I bite my lip as I sit up.

"A little not sexy? I may never be able to look at your clit the same way again." He shuts my Kindle off and sets it on the chair I just vacated as I straddle his lap. I rub myself over him. I can feel the zipper of his jeans through the thin fabric of my barely there purple bikini, and it makes me crave what's underneath.

Taking my hint, Matt wastes no time unzipping and unbuttoning his jeans. He arches into me with a low growl as he pushes them down below his hips, freeing his beautiful dick. I love how Matt can read what I want without me having to say anything.

I take him in both of my hands and stroke slowly. I twist my wrists as I stroke, running my thumb over the sensitive place just below his tip I've come to learn drives him so crazy that he nearly comes within seconds. He closes his eyes and leans his head back while I work him.

Each stroke makes him harder and harder. My favorite thing in the world to do is please him. However I can, and as often as he both needs and wants it. His soft moans and sighs are how I know I'm doing everything right. The way his hips move with my pace and his dick thrusts up and down in my hands to the rhythm of my strokes.

I shift and move down between his legs. I close my eyes and moan around him when I take him in my mouth. "Mmm… Matt…"

His fingers tangle in my hair, and he bobs my head up and down at the speed he wants it. "Fuck, Lyric." He looks down at me and meets my eyes as his grip tightens. The soft smile he gives me is his way of telling me to not stop.

"Mmm…" My teeth lightly scrape up his shaft as he moves my head up and down. My tongue swirls around his tip every time I reach it before he thrusts his dick back into my mouth and pushes my head down. I love when he takes control and makes me do everything he needs me to.

"I'm gonna come, baby." He pushes me down so his dick is just touching the back of my throat and comes. His hot liquid spills from him down my throat.

I moan as I swallow, slowing my strokes as he comes. "Mmm…" I suck and lick him clean, pleased when his grip loosens in my hair, and he falls limp back on the chair. "My favorite snack."

He tugs me up so I'm straddling him again and kisses me deeply. His hands run up my thighs to the strings of my bikini bottoms. He unties them and tugs them off, tossing them aside. He grips my hips and buries himself balls deep inside my pussy.

"Fuck, how are you still so tight after all the times I've fucked you?" He looks up at me as he tugs the ties on my top. He throws it as my tits spill out for him. He buries his head in them as he grips my ass and starts lifting me off him. He slams me back down as he nips and sucks at my nipples.

"Oh my God! Matt!" I grip his shoulders and arch into him. He slaps my ass with both hands making me jerk on his dick. He takes turns sucking hard at my nipples while he slams me down on him again and again. I twist my hips as he thrusts into me with every slam.

He kisses up my neck, nipping at the sensitive flesh. He scrapes his teeth over it as soon as I tilt my head, giving him more access. He bites it gently and sucks hard. He licks and kisses it with a low growl.

"All mine."

"Yours! All yours!" I crush my mouth to his as I dig my fingers into his hair. He tangles one of his hands in my hair and thrusts harder, faster, and deeper into me. He deepens the kiss, starting an intoxicating jive with my tongue.

I press my body against his, molding myself to him, unable to get close enough. I press my tits against his chest and slow the pace slightly, moving slowly over his dick before slamming myself down on him. I repeat the motion over and over, clenching my pussy tightly around him each and every time until my thighs begin to shake, and my pussy pulses and clenches uncontrollably, begging him to let me come.

Matt buries himself inside me again, holding me down. "Holy fuck, Lyric. Come for me, baby."

"Ah! Matt!" I come hard for him, collapsing against him as our hips quake together.

"God, Lyric," he groans into my hair as he slides slowly in and out of me as he comes. He's making a complete mess with both of our come, but I don't care.

We gasp and pant and moan and hum together as we hold each other close while we come down from our high. We tremble and shiver, our hands unable to stop touching one another. I love this time as much as the sex. Just being with him, connected like this, is all I need sometimes. And somehow, he picks up on every single moment that I need that extra time. I'll never understand it, but I'm forever grateful he can read me so well.

(Two Months Later)

"Are you going to tell me where we're going?" I ask Matt, sticking close to his side and holding his arm. I have a black silk tie over my eyes and tied around my head. I've been blindfolded like this for the past two hours. My voice echoes in my ears because he also has noise canceling headphones on my ears. I can't hear or see anything.

He moves the headphones off my ears. "Nope. I'm not. But I promise I'll take the blindfold and the headphones off soon. Little longer, baby."

I pout as he puts the headphones over my ears. He kisses my pout, so I pout more to get more kisses. He smothers me in them until I'm giggling.

I've been with Matt for about six months now. And they've been the most amazing six months of my life. I can't believe it's already been four months since I left. Since I thought he didn't want me. I still can't quite figure out what made me think that I'd ever survive not having him in my life. I don't know how I would have managed not having Mariah or DJ. How I could have managed not having Brody's advice. Tyler is great, but he can't take the place of all of them. Especially Matt.

No one can.

A few minutes later, Matt is leading me somewhere else. He puts his hands on my hips and steers me somewhere before he stops, then tugs me next to him. He puts what I think is a seatbelt on me and tightens it before pulling me into his side and keeping an arm around me.

I relax against him. It's not that I don't trust him. I do. But if he's not touching me, or I can't feel him, I start to panic. Not being able to see or hear anything is one of the scariest things I think I've ever been through. It gives me an entirely new perspective on the seeing and hearing impaired people of the world.

I impatiently wait until I feel myself moving. "Matt, I know I'm in a plane. Please can we take the blindfold and headphones off?"

He gently pulls one of the ears for the headphones off. "Baby, trust me. I really want you to be surprised. Not much longer." He replaces the headphones and kisses me again. I give up the fight and lean against him. Soon, I feel us taking off. My stomach lurches. I grab his hand and melt into the safety of his embrace.

★★★

"Matt? Please let me out of this blindfold and take off the headphones. I've been this way for hours upon hours."

"Little bit longer," he says after he removes the headphones to speak, then replaces them. I nearly cry.

"At the risk of sounding whiny, I feel like I've been in them for hours. Minus the little bit of time on the plane. How you afforded a private jet, I'll never understand." He doesn't answer me, but he does squeeze my hand. A few minutes later, he leads me somewhere else and up something. I sniffle. "Matt…"

He squeezes my hand, then stops after a few more steps. He takes the headphones off and kisses my neck as he starts to untie the blindfold. "Ready, pretty girl?"

"So ready." I sniffle again and lean back into him. He finishes untying the blindfold and removes it. I blink a few times to let my eyes adjust to the light and am in complete awe of the enchanting vision in front of me. "Oh… God…"

There's blue water as far as the eye can see. Lush, green landscape fused with ice glaciers and snowy peaks surrounds us. There are people gathered near the hull of the ship next to us pointing at something. I try to

119

follow their gestures, but I'm overwhelmed by everything else. There's so much to see.

Matt kisses my neck and holds me close to him. My back is firmly against his chest. He rests his chin on my shoulder as he sways with me. "Figured out where you are yet?"

I take a closer look around me, trying to figure it out, but my mind can't seem to focus on just one thing. I shake my head. "I've figured out I'm on a boat."

He chuckles. "Good start." He kisses my neck. I can't help but close my eyes. "Oh, shit! Look at that!"

My eyes snap open, and I look where he's pointing. "Oh my God!" I see the blowhole of a giant whale before it dives back under the water. It surfaces again moments later blowing a fountain of water into the air. "Oh my God!" I bounce and wiggle excitedly as I watch. Two smaller whales join in the fun. I squeal. "Matt! Look at that! It's a family!"

I can feel him smile against my neck. "What do you think?"

"It's so beautiful. So, so beautiful. I don't even care where we are. I'm just so, so happy." I wrap my arms around his as he sways with me as the boat we're on rocks gently.

We stay like that until the boat pulls away from the dock and begins its journey to its unknown destination just as the sun begins to set. It's only then that I question why we're the only ones standing on the hull. The other boat had lots of people standing and watching the whales. I bite my lip as I look up at Matt questioningly.

He smiles as he kisses me softly. "What, pretty girl?"

I blush, but don't know why. "I love when you call me that." I snuggle against him. "I was just curious... We're the only ones on the hull of the boat... And you haven't let me see anything other than what's in front of us..."

"Mmhmm..."

"So... Why are there no other people on the boat?"

"Well... To answer that... I need you to close your eyes."

I pout as cutely as possible. "No..."

He chuckles. "Yes. This time it'll just be a few seconds."

I sigh. "Okay." I close my eyes. "Ready."

"Good girl. Keep them closed for me," he whispers in my ear. I shiver and smile at his praise. I don't know why he makes me so incredibly giddy when he says things like 'good girl' or telling me how well I did at something. It's like the submissive in me that I never really let out or let show to anyone but him is blossoming.

"Promise." He turns me around and steers me somewhere. After a few steps, he stops. I feel his arms circle my waist tightly once more.

"Open your eyes," he whispers in my ear.

I do as he tells me and open them slowly. I squeak and throw my hands over my mouth. "Oh my God!" I run to Mariah and squeeze her tightly. I run to DJ and hug him. He lifts me off the ground. Brody and Tyler each hug me just as tightly as I hug them. "What are you guys doing here? How did you get here?"

"We were on the same plane as you," DJ says. "We all chipped in and rented it and this yacht."

"The same plane?" I look at him incredulously. "How is that possible? It's not like it was that big."

"You know that curtain across the back wall? I told you that was where the flight staff got the drinks and everything?"

I tilt my head and furrow my brows as I look up at Matt. "Yes…"

"Well, I wasn't entirely honest. They do get the drinks and prepare food back there, but that's also where they were. We cut off damn near half the plane from you. Bathrooms were back there. I was pretty grateful there was one in front, too." Matt sits down on the couch in the middle of the yacht and gestures to his lap.

I don't hesitate. His lap is one of my favorite places in the world. I immediately obey and sit, curling up between his legs as he wraps his arms around my waist. "I can't believe you did all of this," I say quietly looking down at my fingers as everyone settles around us.

"I'd do anything for you, honey. And I know you've always wanted to see a wolf. Not easily seen where we live," he teases.

I smile brightly. "Oh my God! Will I really get to see a wolf do you think? From a yacht?"

"According to this brochure," Tyler says. "You can even see a mountain goat."

I giggle. "That would be a sight to see."

Brody leans over. "Damn. It says there are killer whales here."

"We have killer whales at SeaWorld," DJ reminds him.

"I know, but this is in their natural habitat and not a giant tank."

I smile as Brody and everyone launch into the thing they want to see the most. Mariah is most excited about seeing sea otters. DJ really wants to see a bald eagle swoop down and pluck a fish right out of the water. Tyler wants to see a moose. And Matt, for reasons I can't quite understand, is convinced he will see a salmon as big as he is. Considering how big he is… I doubt that's going to happen.

We all talk long into the night, enjoying our time together. I'm so excited Tyler is here, I haven't seen him in what feels like forever to me. I've missed the man I've considered a father. Brody is amazing, but doesn't quite fit the large shoes Tyler does in my world.

Matt kisses my neck. "Baby, let's go out to the deck. I have a surprise for you."

I smile softly as I blink a few times to stay awake. "Okay."

He nudges me off him and takes my hand, leading me out to the deck. I shiver slightly in the cool breeze, but when he wraps me in his jacket, the chill is instantly gone. He puts an arm around me, and I lean into him.

"If you look up there…" He points to a cliff. The yacht quietly bobs on the water, as we've anchored for the night. I look up to the cliff he's pointing at. "You'll see something that I think might make you happy."

I focus on the cliff. It's a little difficult to do in the dark, but after my eyes adjust, I realize the moonlight reflecting off the water and shining down from the sky lights up the cliffs perfectly. Matt kisses the side of my head as he takes a step back. I keep looking, eagerly seeking my prize, though I have no idea what it is.

I tilt my head and squint a little. "What is it?"

"Keep looking baby. According to the yacht's captain, something exciting happens every single night about this time on that cliff."

I bite my lip, bouncing in elation. It's not long before I see what he's talking about. Tears spring to my eyes. "Oh my God… Oh my God!" My eyes widen as I watch in fascination at the scene unfolding in front of me.

Wolf after wolf after wolf line up on the edge of the cliff. They look up at the moon before they look around, seemingly seeking out any danger. Then they all start howling at the moon. One by one.

"They say wolves don't do what they are. They travel in a pack, sure, but they never all come to the same place and howl like that. Taking turns. Wolves like their privacy. Howling at the moon is something most say wolves do because it's part of their nature," Matt explains. "But the truth is, that's not why they do it."

I don't take my eyes off the wolves. Instead, I watch the ritual. My heart nearly feels as if it's breaking, but I don't know why. "Why do they do it? It sounds so…" I don't really know the words.

"Sad?" Matt finishes for me.

"Yeah. Sad."

"Well, wolves howl because they're trying to find a lost love. Or a lost member of their pack. They do it because they're trying to help that lost wolf find their way home. The locals here believe that these particular wolves have all lost their soulmate. Wolves mate for life. So when they lose their mate, they typically won't ever find another one. Most wolves don't survive the loss. It's believed that these wolves are howling to find their lost love. To help them come home."

I reach up and wipe a tear from my eye as I turn to him when the wolves finish their stunning display of love. Matt is on one knee holding up a ring. I gasp as I look at him with watery eyes. "Matt?"

"I don't want another mate, baby. I only want you. I'll do anything to bring you home if you ever stray too far. I'll do anything to protect you. To lead you. Guide you. I'll spend my entire life making your place at my side feel like home. Marry me. Make me the happiest man in the world and be the woman who not only keeps me on my toes, but keeps me fighting. Keeps me loving and honest."

I can do nothing but nod. I barely register the ring he slides on my finger. Or the cheers of my family around me. The only thing that matters to me is Matt. His arms around me. The happiness he exudes in his tight hug as he lifts me off the ground and spins me around.

Matt.

My everything.

My world.

123

Epilogue

☆ Matt ☆

(Six Months Later)

I scrub my hands down my face and look out at the crystal clear water below me. Lyric and I have been together for a year now. It's been six months since I proposed to her on the yacht just below the cliff I'm standing on. Being with her has been the best time of my life. I fall more and more in love with her every single day.

We've been through a lot together, and as I look out at the horizon, I can't help but be grateful for all of it. It's all created this unbreakable bond between us. The undeniable attraction that led to this overwhelming need I have to be her greatest protector… The strength she showed facing down Hamilton, even though I know how terrified she was to do it…

I smile as DJ appears at my side and claps a hand on my shoulder. "You ready to say goodbye to the bitter asshole you used to be?"

I laugh. "I'm pretty damn sure the asshole in me isn't going anywhere."

"Wouldn't expect it to. But the bitter part of you? She took a grenade and destroyed all of that. Left no trace."

"I haven't let myself get close to a woman after what happened when I was younger. I think it scared me so fucking badly, I refused to allow myself to fall. Didn't want to hurt her."

"Probably didn't want to get hurt yourself."

"More like… struggled to trust myself. When you nearly kill someone, and then that person does nothing… No charges. No police report. Not even a text or phone call after you've apologized numerous fucking times. It messes with you. Makes you question yourself in ways that I can't even describe. I built up walls and reinforced all of them just to make sure no one got in."

"I don't know about no one. You got pretty close to me. Brody. Fuck, even Mariah. Sometimes, I think you like her more than me."

I nod and smile. "I do like her more than you. She's nicer to look at."

He laughs. "Don't touch my girl, you fucker."

"Seriously, though. I have a very small circle. And I was okay with that. Then Lyric comes along and makes me wonder if all of that protection I built up around myself to keep myself from hurting anyone else was just somehow my way of keeping everyone away from me. Everyone but her. Like I was just waiting for her to save me or something."

"And here I thought you were the one doing the saving," he teases.

"Fuck. She doesn't need anyone to save her. She doesn't need anyone at all. She's the strongest person I've ever met."

"I don't know about that. I mean, yeah. She's strong. But I think she's strong because of you. You give her that strength, Matt. Just like she gives you yours."

I look over at him a little curiously. "You think so?"

He smiles, but doesn't look at me. "Do you remember when Mariah first started at the department? How timid she was?"

I look back out over the water. "I didn't think there was any fucking way she'd make it on the force."

"And then you went on that first call with her. You couldn't believe that quiet strength she has. You came to me that night and said Mariah is going to make one fuck of a cop. You couldn't wait to be there to see it."

"I was right."

125

"Yeah. You were right. But what you didn't know then was that she had that confidence because of you. I know she didn't tell you that until later. And I know she also told you that more and more of her ability to fight through her own demons and be the best she can is because of me. Truth is, it's the same for me. I'd be nothing without her. It's the same thing with you and Lyric." He looks over at me a moment before looking back over the water. "Neither of you would be who you are without each other. So don't ever doubt what you bring to the table. She needs you just as much as you've come to need her. Without her?" He smiles as he turns and heads back towards wherever it is he conjured himself from. "You'd still be that bitter asshole."

I laugh because I know he's right. Everyone always tells me that Lyric herself has toned down. She's not as wild as she was. Reckless. Irresponsible. And that it's because of me. Truth is, the girl tamed me. Not the other way around. I'd walk through that department like a terror sometimes because I was pissed off at the world. Cynical. Maybe I still am a little but nowhere near what I was.

Lyric saved me.

I glance up as the sky starts taking on different colors and glance at my watch.

It's time.

Time to begin my life with the most beautiful woman inside and out that I've ever had the honor of knowing.

I take my place on the left side of the altar as everyone settles in their seats. DJ takes his place next to me, giving my arm a reassuring squeeze. I'm still fairly convinced Lyric is going to realize what she's gotten herself into and run. Everyone knows she can do better than me.

I watch as Mariah makes her way up the aisle. The light purple halter style dress she's wearing billows gently around her in the Alaskan breeze. Her hair is down for once. A very rare sight, but one most all of us who are close to her revel a little in. Something about her long hair free always makes her look a little more beautiful. A little more carefree.

The purple lilies she carries in her bouquet match the lily DJ and I have pinned to our black suit jackets. The color matches the deep purple of our vests. The chairs that hold our family and friends, many from the department, are covered in a silky purple fabric with a silver bow.

Purple. The color of royalty. My Queen's favorite color.

Because she loves me and wants this wedding to be both of ours, she's somehow incorporated blue into the decor. Blue and white baby's breath accentuates the altar, the bouquets, and even the flowers pinned to our lapels. The side of Mariah's hair is pinned up with a clip that has a purple lily and blue and white baby's breath hanging down into her hair.

Blue.

Representative of a new beginning to me. A signal of starting over. With Hamilton in prison for a long time and all of the shit with him and his obsession behind us, that's exactly what this is.

I have to smile a little thinking of Hamilton Prescott. I have to hand it to the guy. He certainly paved his own way. After we arrested him, we found out so many things about him that it made my head spin. Lyric couldn't keep up.

We found out he was cut off completely from his family. They helped him go into hiding after what he did to Lyric. After that, Hamilton was forced to make his own way. We knew he had the car theft ring going. We did not know that he was also street car racing. We didn't realize that he was stealing these cars and sending them to chop shops before selling them. We had a feeling he was changing vin numbers. But we didn't know he was replacing entire vehicles with parts from vehicles he'd stolen.

His obsession with Lyric, though. That's what scared all of us. We knew the obsession was there, but we didn't know he'd planned on kidnapping her and taking her to Russia. We would have had no chance of getting her back through any kind of legal channels. But we'd all decided if that had happened, we would have torn Russia apart to get to her.

Piece by piece.

All of us.

But none of that matters now. He was charged and convicted of car theft and the kidnapping plot as well as the stalking of Lyric. He was killed in prison by a gang member that he looked at the wrong way. Trying to be tougher than he was. I can't even say I feel bad. Might make me a terrible person, but I know Lyric is safe. She's my priority.

I look down the aisle as Lyric's music starts. I smile at her song choice. I can't get over how perfectly it fits her as I listen to the lyrics she chose as she walks towards me with a soft smile on her face.

I am not afraid anymore. Standing in the eye of the storm. Ready to face this. Dying to taste this sick, sweet warmth. I am not afraid anymore. I want what you got in store. I'm ready to feed now. Get in your seat now… And touch me like you never. And push me like you never. And touch me like you never. 'Cause I am not afraid, I am not afraid anymore. No, no, no.

Lyric meets my eyes as Halsey sings how she's not afraid. I wipe a tear away. With how much she's been through, and how far she's come in trusting me, the lyrics are stunningly accurate.

Stunning. Just like she is.

The long, white, ankle length dress has straps that are around an inch in width. I begged her to get a strapless dress that has a plunging neckline because I love how sexy my girl is, but she overruled me hardcore. She told me she needs the straps to protect her from spilling out of the dress. I definitely wouldn't have minded seeing that, but I'm possessive as fuck. So the plunging neckline was nixed in the ass. I don't want anyone seeing what my girl only gives to me.

We compromised a little. The neckline does plunge slightly, though. And after the alterations, it fits her perfectly. It flows down her body and swells just slightly from her waist. When the breeze hits, it looks like she's floating to me.

But my favorite part about the dress is the light purple ribbon that runs just underneath her tits and ties in the back. The ribbon drops all the way down the length of her dress. The color matches Mariah's dress and our lilies to a tee. Lyric is detail-oriented. Nothing gets past her when it comes to wedding decor and colors. Fuck. Nothing gets by her in any other aspect of our lives either. My girl is truly one of a kind.

I take her hands in mine when she reaches me. She smiles up at me shyly. "Hi."

"Hey there, pretty girl. Ready to make an honest man of me?"

She blushes and looks down, meeting my eyes submissively through her lashes. "I can't wait to marry you."

I squeeze her hands. "I love you, Lyric."

"I love you, too," she whispers.

"Take good care of our daughter," Brody says to me.

"We know how to make sure your body is never found," Tyler says as seriously as possible. I can hear the tease in his voice, though.

I smile as they both pat my shoulder. They turn and head for their seats. I'd been so focused on Lyric that the two of them walking her down the aisle and giving her away to me was something I barely noticed until their voices hit my ears.

Lyric and I both turn to the officiant, keeping our hands locked together, as the officiant begins his speech. I continuously run my thumb soothingly over Lyric's nervously shaking hands until she eventually relaxes. When the time finally comes to put my ring on her finger, it's my turn to have slightly shaky hands. She smiles tenderly and lovingly, the one she reserves just for me, and I'm instantaneously calm.

Before I know it, we've said our vows and made our promise to love one another. Just as the officiant is about to tell me I can kiss my bride, I stop him. I reach up and cup Lyric's face, running my thumb over her bottom lip. She leans into me with slightly closed eyes and parts her lips just enough for me to wish she'd lick my thumb.

I shake my head slightly and take her hands in mine. "Before he announces us, there's something I wanted to say. When we got engaged, I was telling you the story of the wolves that gather here every night. How they're looking for their long lost loves. Or the missing piece of them. How they mate for life." I take out a silver necklace from my pocket. The charm is a wolf howling. I slip it over her neck. "Wolves have always been a part of our relationship. I know how much you like them. You know how much I do. I love all of the drawings you've made of them and let me have framed so I can show them off around our home."

She looks at it with tears in her eyes. "Matt... God, it's so pretty."

I smile at her obvious love for it. "Just like the wolf, you're the only one for me, Lyric. I'll never love another."

"You'll never have the chance to," she whispers shyly as she blushes.

I smile as I lean down, stopping just before her lips. Without taking my eyes off hers, I say, "Now you can tell me I can kiss my bride."

The officiant laughs and announces us to everyone as my lips meet hers. I kiss her deeply, pulling her as close to me as I possibly can. I dip my tongue into her mouth, teasing hers with mine. She submits to me, just like she knows I love, and melts into my kiss. When I pull away, we're both a little dazed.

As we turn to our family and friends, Lyric still securely in my arms, we hear it.

Silence falls as we all listen.

In the distance, one by one, the wolves start howling at the moon that's risen over us. You'd think we'd all be a little scared. After all, we're all on the cliff they usually come to. But we're not. How can we be afraid of something who just wants his love by his side?

Lyric cuddles into me as we all listen. When it's over, we all start walking to our rented vehicles. DJ helps Mariah into ours. I help Lyric. As I shut the door and turn, I meet his eyes. The majestic creature hidden beyond the trees. I can't prove it, but I swear the black wolf nods.

In approval?

I'm not sure. But I smile and nod back as he turns and trots away.

I'll take that as my sign.

Lyric is my life.

My mate.

My forever.

The End

Next in The Beautiful Dream Series

The sweet and sinfully sexy Beautiful Dream Series continues with *Undercover Temptations*.

Most people think I have a pretty good head on my shoulders. I have a good job. I'm a Sergeant with the Gainesville Police Department. I'm a commander on the SWAT team. I'm a single dad. I work hard to make sure my son has everything I didn't.

I've never complained. I put my head down and push through whatever I face because everything I do is for my son.

But I have a secret. A secret I fear could destroy everything I've worked for. I've done very well at hiding it behind a carefully crafted persona. No one knows what I keep hidden.

Until I'm sent on an undercover mission with my best friend.

Lieutenant Matt Chance. The man owns my heart and doesn't even know it.

I try to keep my feelings private, but when he becomes the target of the cunning serial killer we're trying to take down, I'll do everything I need to do to protect him.

Even if it destroys me in the process.

Order *Undercover Temptations* Today!

The Beautiful Dream Series

Available Now

Loving You
My Love, My Heart
Softening Lyric
Undercover Temptations
Captain Charming
Breaking Boundaries
Crashing Into You
Tactical Inferno
Ravishing Our Queen
Cherished By The Texan
Unveiling Our Passions

Box Sets Available

The Beautiful Dream Series: Box Set: Part 1
The Beautiful Dream Series: Box Set: Part 2

Other Books By Melony Ann
The Crane Family Series

Available Now

The Reluctant Mafia King
Sweet Lies
Billion Dollar Love Story
Be Mine
Protecting Her
Dangerously Forbidden Love
His Heart
Love In The Dark

Box Sets Available

The Crane Family Series

The Deimos Trilogy

Available Now

Connor's Legacy
Aryan's Alpha
Kade's Redemption

Box Sets Available

The Deimos Trilogy

The Forbidden Temptation Series

Available Now

The Detective's Forbidden Temptation
The Running Back's Forbidden Temptation

The Lucinio Family Series

Available Now

Rising From The Ashes
The Player's Rebel
Encrypting My Heart
Fighting My Fate

Multi Author Series
Piper Falls: Firehouse 49

Available Now

Ignite My Fire by Melony Ann
Regain My Fire by Kindra White
Playing With My Fire by D.L. Howe
Fight My Fire by Darley Collins
Against My Fire by Anneke Boshoff
Relight My Fire by Louise Murchie
Harness My Fire by Ayana Lisbet
Quench My Fire by Havana Wilder

Let's Be Friends

Follow me on

Bookbub

Facebook

Goodreads

Instagram

Tik Tok

Visit my website
www.melonyannauthor.com

Subscribe to my newsletter and get a FREE never-seen-before NOVELLA
just for subscribers!
https://www.melonyannauthor.com/exclusive-content

Join my Facebook Reader Group!
Melony Ann's Sizzling Book Nook
https://www.facebook.com/groups/melonyannssizzlingbooknook

The official Beautiful Dream Series Playlist on YouTube
https://youtube.com/playlist?list=PLGEiD5wbQmDe1z4_FeeKbMLcBkOz
1M4L4

Dedication

Wolves mate for life. To our loves. Our mates. Our hearts.

Acknowledgements

Brad - I don't know where to begin with you sometimes. You always know just what to say or do. I sometimes have no words to express how much I love you, or how grateful I am to you for all you've done and continue to do for me. I feel like you sacrifice so much sometimes to make sure that me and Laura have the wind we need to sail.

Laura - When I feel like my world is falling apart, you always find a way to be the air I don't think I'm getting enough of. I can never thank you for everything that you do for me, and I can never put how much I love you into the right words. Probably because they haven't been invented yet.

Jay - I sometimes think that the sun will never come up. That I'm drowning. That I'm fighting a darkness that I don't even recognize. But you do. Because of you and our loves, a little more light appears in my world. And I feel like I'm okay again. I love you. So much.

Anneke – You're honestly so incredible. Thank you so much for everything you do.

Jason – I didn't ask you for you. But here you are.

Kayla – Thank you for making sure I'm still standing after so much shit.

To the Bookstagram Community.

To my family.

To all of those who believe in me and support me.

To all of those who don't.

Cover by: Carter Cover Designs

Edited by: Alyssa Skaggs

About Melony Ann

Melony Ann began writing short stories and poetry as a child. She continued honing her craft over the years until she took the plunge and began publishing her work, despite having severe anxiety.

Melony writes contemporary romance stories that are full of suspense and a lot of steam.

When she isn't writing, she is loving her family and working to make her life something she deserves.

Melony believes that if her writing can inspire just one person, then all of her hard work is worth it.

Her hope is that her writing allows each and every one of her readers to escape for a little while. To dive into a different world one book at a time.